Praise For The Destination: Desire Series

"I loved this amazing, emotional love story... A tear or two became commonplace during some intense scenes. In Ms. Jordan's talented hands, the characters evolved naturally and realistically, flaws and all." *-Harlequin Junkie Reviews*

"5 stars. My favorite in the series so far. I just loved the back story of this couple and it's just a different twist on a romance. Loved it!" *-Kristi Simonsen*

"This is an well written story, where you get invested in the characters and root for them to have their HEA...I cannot wait to see what comes next in this series. 5 stars" *-Gigi Staub*

"This was a fabulous story with great characters... one of the best I've read this year. I LOVED this." *-Jennifer McKenzie*

GETTING IT RIGHT

DESTINATION: DESIRE

BOOK 5

C. JORDAN

CJ BOOKS

contents

DEDICATION

For all my readers who read Tate and Karen's romance, met Tate's little sister, and loved Laurel enough to want to see her happily ever after.

For Orchid, who boldly stated that she wanted to be someone's gay awakening. That line just had to be immortalized.

Also for Melissa, Julia, and Sharon—women who know the value of many knives, prayer mafias, and a well-timed, "You need Jesus!"

CHαPTer one

Half Moon Bay, California

"Thanks for lending me a hand, Ben." Laurel Patton stepped back, propped her fists on her hips, and surveyed their handiwork. She stood in the middle of her brother and sister-in-law's living room, looking at a pair of paintings hanging over their couch. One had been there for years, the second was a gift for their eleventh anniversary.

"No problem." Her sister-in-law's younger brother grinned conspiratorially, dimples digging deep grooves into his cheeks.

Ben had helped her sneak into the house while Tate and Karen were out. The two collaborators had hauled the sizeable canvas in from Laurel's car and positioned the pieces so they hung evenly on the wall.

Her original watercolor of Positano on the Amalfi Coast of Italy had captured the way the town's pastel buildings layered up the side of a cliff like a fancy wedding cake. It was where Tate had first introduced the Patton family to Karen, and where he'd proposed to her. Beside it now hung a painting of the house the couple had bought and restored a few years back—a gingerbread-laden Victorian mansion perched on a bluff over the Pacific Ocean. Laurel had tried to evoke the same style and palette, so that the two canvases were obviously meant to be a pair. Since she didn't work with watercolor very often anymore, it had been a nice challenge to her artistic skills.

She tilted her head and eyed her work critically. Not too bad. The first painting was done while she was taking a watercolor class as part of her Fine Arts degree from the Rhode Island School of Design. She'd loved her years at RISD, and trying to recapture that frame of mind for the new canvas had taken her back to those times.

Ben bumped his shoulder against hers. "They're going to love it. It blows my gift to them out of the water."

"Thanks." She winked. "I like kicking everyone else's ass with my awesomeness."

He snorted. "Your modesty slays me."

"You're welcome." She turned to walk into the kitchen, going to the fridge for a bottle of water. It was probably her last chance to get anything before the catering company took over for the anniversary party that night.

Ben followed and settled back against the enormous island, shoving his hands in his suit pockets. He looked every inch the ambitious young lawyer now, but he'd still been in his gawky tween years the first time they'd met.

All grown up now, he'd just passed his bar exam and joined her brother's firm the month before, and she'd bet Ben would be stellar in the courtroom with his resonant bass voice that could rival James Earl Jones. Considering his voice had cracked on every other word for the first few years after they'd been introduced, she'd been pleasantly surprised his tone had deepened so much. No one wanted a squeaky-voiced lawyer defending them.

She waved her bottle at him. "What did you get our siblings?"

He cocked his head. "It sounds a little incestuous when you say *our* siblings, even if it is technically correct."

"What did you get my brother and sister-in-law, aka your sister and brother-in-law?" She rolled her eyes. "It was faster my way."

"A date night while I babysit Nick. They get gift certificates for a movie and dinner at their favorite restaurant."

Pursing her lips, she nodded. "That's a pretty good gift. I think any couple with a rambunctious toddler would love that."

"Yeah, but it's not a piece of art from a famous painter." He widened his eyes as if to indicate any idiot would agree with him.

"Pfft. Fame is relative. I'm not exactly Van Gogh."

"Says the woman who got invited to be an artist-in-residence at The Creative Enclave." He wagged a finger at her. "Don't think Tate wasn't bragging about you after you told him that."

She felt a rush of heat hit her cheeks. Her, Laurel Patton, blushing. There was a novel experience. Of course, she blew any semblance of modesty by offering a cocky grin and throwing her hands up in victory. "I am a badass, what can I say?"

"Tate pulled up their website and read the list of names for artists who've been part of their program." He gave a low whistle. "You're in some august company there."

"Some of my idols have been artist-in-residence for The Enclave. Okay...the idols who were around during the last century. I have some that have been dead since the Renaissance." She took a swig of water. "It'll be a whole summer of painting. Plus, I get to mentor an up-and-coming painter too. I've taught a few art classes over the years, but never individual mentoring. It should be fun. Unless they're an asshole, in which case I will make their lives miserable for three months. Because: homework."

"That's the spirit." He winked. "Always have a strategy for winning."

"I like winning," she agreed. Part of the fun of this trip was that she would get to spend time with other artists. Not just painters, but sculptors, potters, photographers, videographers, writers...you name it. She liked the idea of having that kind of community, at least for a while. Painting was a pretty solitary profession.

"When do you leave?"

"Tate's driving me to SFO in the morning. I just have to survive this party." She couldn't hold in a deep sigh, some of her excitement fizzling away.

"Your parents are coming, huh?" Sympathy reflected in his gaze.

"Let's be honest. It'll be just my mother. Daddy Dearest isn't taking the time to come to a party with no political gain. The guest list isn't A-list enough."

Ben winced, but didn't deny it. They both knew Robert Patton had worked Tate like a dog for years, trying to remake his son in his image, and it had nearly cost Tate his marriage. Laurel was grateful her brother had seen the light of day before he's lost the best thing that had ever happened to him. Karen was an absolute gem. Laurel had liked her on sight, somehow knowing this woman would be the only thing Tate loved more than the law. Well, now he had Karen, little Nick, and then the law. Which was how it should be.

Ben injected a note of cheer into his voice. "Well, my parents will both be here and they rock."

"I know, you lucky bastard," she groused.

He just laughed.

Dear God, she was going to have to deal with her mother. The two of them always brought out the absolute worst in each other.

Francesca, the obnoxious socialite who insisted her daughter marry the right sort of man, and Laurel, whose inner rebellious teen came out with claws bared.

"I notice you got your hair dyed again." Ben's grin turned wicked. "I like the turquoise streaks—very fluorescent. Your mom's going to love it."

"Yep." She fluffed her long tresses, not bothering to deny that needling her mother had been part of the decision-making process for refreshing her always colorful hair. She'd done green, blue, purple, fire engine red...pick a neon shade. It was her signature now. Sometimes she did streaks and sometimes she dyed only the tips. One time, she'd done just the left side of her head bright pink. Francesca's eyeballs had nearly exploded out of their sockets when she'd seen the effect. Watching the apoplectic reaction had been awesome. Laurel grinned at the memory. "Let the games begin."

Three hours later, Laurel wanted to kill herself. No, she wanted to kill Francesca. Slowly, and in painfully inventive ways.

Because her mother hadn't come alone, as it turned out. No, she'd brought along every young, single male associate in Robert Patton's law firm. They were all from very good families, naturally. Families that belonged to Robert and Francesca's country club.

In other words, they were the right sort of men. An entire herd of them. She was stuck in a group of them making small talk, and they kept taking turns giving her once-overs—alternating between staring at either her hair or her breasts. Her chest wasn't that impressive, but she now wished she'd worn a turtleneck rather than a slinky, low-cut top. She felt her eyelid begin to twitch and took a deep swig of her wine, longing for something a whole lot stronger. Tequila shots sounded good.

One of the lawyers gave her slightly condescending smile while he swirled and sniffed his vino. "So you're an...artist?"

"Painter." She forced a pleasant grin, calculating how she might make her next escape. She'd slipped away from this group four times now, but Francesca was on a mission. She had the tenacity of a pit bull with lockjaw. Laurel's hand tightened on the stem of her glass. "I work primarily with oil, but I also do some mixed media."

If anything, the man's expression became even more patronizing. "Ah, that's nice. My mother toys with ceramics a bit."

How many times had Laurel been accused of being a dilettante? It was true she'd always had a trust fund to fall back on, and that fact hadn't exactly endeared her to other artists who'd struggled and starved to make ends meet before they achieved success. Never mind that she'd worked her ass off to gain recognition for her work. No, her family had money, so this was just a hobby, a phase that she'd get over. Right.

Her teeth locked together, and it took effort not to snarl. "Well, I'm not toying. This is how I make my living."

The way Francesca patted Laurel's shoulder reminded her of how one soothed an overexcited terrier. Great. Just great. Her mother's laugh tinkled out. "But I'd love to see her more settled so she doesn't have worry about making a living."

Settled? That was rich. Francesca might have been married for forty years, but she'd screwed her way through every tennis instructor, golf pro, and pool boy at the country club. Robert annually took his pick of the new first-year female law associates at his firm. The Patton parental units weren't exactly a glowing example of a healthy relationship. It apparently worked for them, but it would not work for Laurel. She had no desire to be their kind of settled.

Another law-boy broke in, his tone warmer and friendlier than the wine sniffer's. "I imagine you'd love more grandchildren too, Francesca. I see how you dote on young Nick."

"Nicholas is such a dear." The older woman's expression softened with pure adoration.

Laurel had to admit Francesca was a far kinder and more involved grandmother than she had been a mother. She'd also surprised Laurel by supporting Tate when he'd left the Patton family firm and struck out on his own. Unfortunately, the leeway Francesca gave her son never quite translated to her daughter. Then again, Tate had been the golden boy who exceeded all familial expectations for a lot of years, whereas Laurel had been born the defiant black sheep. Her artistic bent meant she'd been the kid finger-painting the walls, the tween wearing wild jewelry, the teen coloring her hair and piercing various body parts. She just needed to experiment and live out loud. Proper Pattons didn't do anything out loud. She just...could never be the daughter her parents wanted.

The only person who had always supported her, loved her, tried to understand her, had been her big brother. It was for him alone that Laurel held her tongue, played nice with Mama Matchmaker and the pack of lawyers, and didn't cause a scene at Tate's anniversary party.

But it was damn tempting, especially when the guys kept looking her over like she was an exotic game animal and they were ready for a safari hunt.

"Excuse me, everyone. I'm sorry to interrupt." Ben's deep voice sounded behind her. "Laurel, would you care to dance?"

"Yes, I'd love to." Okay, maybe she'd agreed a little too fast because her mom's eyes narrowed, but she'd just about exhausted her cocktail party chitchat repertoire.

She grabbed Ben's hand and dragged him out the French doors which led to the huge deck that served as the dance floor. A string quartet sent lovely, lilting classical music floating through the night.

"My mom's trying to marry me off to a lawyer, since she can't make me be one." She sucked in a breath of the fresh, early summer evening air and let it calm some of her tension. Tonight was a celebration—it was supposed to be fun.

Ben pulled her into a loose dance hold, and they moved easily across the floor. "I saw that. She's persistent too."

"Right? She's never gonna give up the dream of me being a country club girl. The very thought makes me want to break out in hives."

He considered that for a moment. "Hives might scare the guys away. Tell them it's an STD."

"I like you so much." She chortled and offered him a sunny smile. "Anyway, thanks for the rescue."

His broad shoulder dipped in a nonchalant shrug. "It would hurt my sister's feelings if she spent the evening scrubbing blood out of the carpet."

"It was a close call there."

"I don't blame you. Those guys look like a bunch of limp dick losers," he observed with characteristic bluntness. "Seriously, they'd marry you to make your daddy like them."

She sniffed. "I have no interest in looking at their dicks to see how limp they are or aren't. And I have no desire to help anyone get into Dad's good graces. I'm not in his good graces. By choice."

He tilted his head. "If it's not broken, don't fix it."

"It works for me." She grinned as he swooped her into a quick turn. "All right, then."

It was nice to dance. She didn't have to worry that she'd say or do the wrong thing and mess up the fete. She hadn't needed to constrain herself so much since she was in high school. Just one more reason to stay away from her parents' world. She didn't fit there, and she didn't want to.

But she didn't want to talk about that anymore. Time for a topic change. "So, Ben…tell me about what's going on between you and the redhead over there."

He didn't pretend not to know who she was talking about. "Nora Kirby."

The woman in question danced by with one of Laurel's husband candidates. She laughed at something the law-boy said, and Ben's expression darkened, but the look he gave Nora was filled with such naked, tormented longing that Laurel felt a bit voyeuristic for witnessing it. Nora seemed to notice the attention and glanced over. The glare she gave Ben was baleful. He winked in return, which made the redhead's face flush with enough fury to match her hair.

"Um…isn't Anne Kirby one of Karen's best friends?"

He dragged his gaze back to Laurel. "Nora's her younger sister."

"And you want to bone her. But she hates your ass."

"That sums up the last decade of my life nicely, yeah." His tone was pleasant, all of that yearning buried deep again.

Because she couldn't help herself, she asked, "What did you do to make her loathe you?"

He sighed. "I was a typical tween jerk then, and she's tried to give me the silent treatment ever since."

She replayed their interaction in her head for a moment. "You antagonize her so, instead of silence, she gives you hissing, spitting hellcat."

"Yeah, plus she's hot when she's mad." His grin was slow and wicked.

Shaking her head, she tried not to laugh. "Your maturity level is dropping by the second."

He shrugged. "Never claimed to be a grown up."

"Yet you represent people in court." She widened her eyes at him.

The night air swirled around them as he swept her into another quick turn. "I was required to pass the bar exam, not a maturity test."

Sucking in her cheeks, she tried to smother a loud guffaw. "Nice, Ben."

The high-pitched squeal of childish laughter drew her gaze. Tate and Karen were dancing, and Nicky was perched in Tate's arms, bouncing gleefully between his parents. Karen glowed with happiness, and Tate had never looked more content. It was good to see them that way. They'd been on the verge of divorce a few years before, but they'd managed to weather the storm together.

"I'm so glad they worked everything out," Ben said quietly, his thoughts obviously following Laurel's.

She nodded. "I'm so glad my brother pulled his head out of his ass in time to save his marriage."

Tate and Karen drifted closer, and Laurel turned toward them. "Up for a little partner swapping?"

Her brother laughed, shaking his head. "Actually, we need to put Nick to bed."

"I'll help Karen do that." Ben wiggled his fingers at the toddler. "Come here, little man."

"Eeee!" Nick hurled himself toward his uncle, who caught the boy easily. "Unca Ben!"

Hooking her arm through her brother's, Karen swept her free hand in front of her. "Lead on. Bedtime stories await."

"Cool." The trio disappeared into the crowd, heading inside the house.

Tate's gaze lingered on his wife as she walked away, blatant love on his face.

"Happiness looks good on you, bro."

He smiled, caught her hand, swiftly twirled her, and dipped her over his arm. "Thanks. Life is fine. Amazingly, outstandingly fine."

"Yeah, yeah." She poked his shoulder. "Rub it in."

Another fancy spin, then he said, "That's what an anniversary party is for, right? Flaunting your marital bliss?"

"That's definitely worth celebrating." And something he hadn't been able to celebrate until recently.

"Yeah." His sigh was heartfelt and loaded with pleasure.

A pang of quiet envy hit her heart as the music changed and she let him lead her around the floor. Not that she wasn't thrilled for Tate and his wife, but she wished she had some of that joy in her life too. As much as she adored her older brother, his wife, and their darling son, being around them reminded her of how...lonely...her life could be. She loved her work, loved that she could travel at the drop of a hat, so her no-strings-attached lifestyle had been fabulous for years. But lately, she'd longed for more. She just didn't know what *more* would look like. She wasn't really a settling down, kids and a white picket fence type of girl, even though that life looked pretty good for her brother. She definitely wasn't interested in her parents' cold, distant excuse for a marriage.

She couldn't help feeling stupid for being so dissatisfied. She had the career she'd gone to college for—her talents were lauded far and wide in her field. That was what she'd always wanted, what she'd worked so hard for. But she was still alone, and maybe...maybe she'd like to be less alone sometimes. None of the men she'd dated had ever inspired her to wish for wedding bells and babies. She'd always thought she'd get around to those things someday, but when would someday finally turn into today? It'd been awhile since she'd bothered with dating, so maybe she should give some lucky guy a chance again.

But then one of Laurel's hubby candidates came waltzing by with her mother.

"If you let her try to change partners, I will kill you. Anniversary or no anniversary." Her voice was low and deadly. Only an idiot would think she was kidding.

Because her brother was a smart man with a healthy sense of self-preservation, he executed a neat turn that moved them away from the other couple. "Sorry she's hounding you tonight. Karen and I didn't know about the flock she was bringing."

"Of course not." She patted his shoulder. "Mom would have known you'd say no."

But seeing Francesca reminded Laurel of one simple fact. There were worse things than being lonely—there was being with the wrong guy. And with her mom on the matchmaking warpath, it was definitely time to get the hell out of Dodge.

Thank God she was hopping on a plane in the morning.

CHAPTER TWO

The Creative Enclave, Colorado

"We've been driving forever. Are we there yet?"

Normally, having a kid ask that question was guaranteed to grate on the nerves, but seeing the excitement on his daughter's face was like a swift kick to Neil's chest. When was the last time Violet had been excited about anything?

Only he knew the answer all too well: not since before her mother—his ex-wife—had died in a car accident over year ago.

Vi had always been mature for her age, but it seemed as if the weight of the world had settled on her narrow shoulders during the last thirteen months. She cried less now than she had at first, but grief was hard, ugly, and awful. Just when you thought things were getting better, it snuck up on you again with a vicious sucker punch. Neil knew all that, had dealt with it himself when he'd lost his father and then his mother, but it didn't help much. He could only try to be there for his baby girl as she worked through this process. Most of the time, he felt like he was floundering, but maybe that was true of any father trying to navigate the teen years with his daughter. All he could do was give Violet his love and support and hope the pain got easier with time.

The airport van rounded a corner, which revealed a break in the dense green forest, and a huge wooden lodge came into view. He pointed. "Yep, I think we're there."

"Cool." A grin tucked a dimple into one cheek, and she glanced over at him, gray eyes wide. "This summer is going to be so dope."

"Of course you'd think that." He nudged her arm. "It was your idea for me to take the residency."

"Well, yeah." She looked down her nose at him. "Like I said...dope."

With a wink, he tweaked her chin.

"I'm so ready to not be sitting, though." She bounced against the confines of her seatbelt.

"You're telling me." Their flight from LA to Denver had been delayed by several hours, and the drive out to The Creative Enclave could only be described as long and bumpy. Plus, his knees were wedged up against the seat in front of him. There were definite disadvantages to being over six feet tall.

He called to the driver, "Stop for a moment at the lodge and let me check us in, then we'll head to the cabin."

"We're in cabin 3B," Vi reminded him. She'd pored over the orientation packet they'd been sent.

The van braked and Neil climbed out. "Yes, but we should let The Enclave staff know we're here."

She wrinkled her nose. "Plus, a key might be useful."

"It might," he agreed solemnly, and she stuck her tongue out at him. "Wait here."

"Aw, man!"

He ignored the whining objection and the way his cramped muscles protested movement. At this point in his very long day, he needed a hot shower, and a beer. Sexual favors from a gorgeous woman wouldn't be unwelcome either, but he was guessing only the first option was within the realm of possibility this evening. He'd take it. He mounted the lodge's short staircase, striding across the porch and into the building. For all its size, the place glowed with homey comfort, all honey-colored wood walls and worn carpet runners.

A young woman stepped out of an office. "Hi, can I help y—oh, you're Neil Graves."

"That's right. I need to check my daughter and me in for the summer program." He mustered a smile. "Are you the person I need to speak to about that?"

"Yes, Mr. Graves. One second." She executed a pirouette, rifled through some files on her desk, and came back with a bulky envelope. She handed it over, and then her hands fluttered in front of her. "I'm Mimi Snodgrass. I'm The Creative Enclave assistant director—well, actually I'm the interim director while my boss is out on maternity leave. Anyway, I adore your books, and I was so thrilled when you accepted the invitation to be an artist-in-residence. I was sure you'd say no."

"Me too." He winked. "You can thank my daughter for talking me into it."

"I will!" She beamed. "There's a cabin key in there for her too, so you don't have to be with her at all times. You're one of our first artists to arrive. We have a meet-and-mingle with all program participants on Sunday at six PM, then we officially start on Monday."

Since it was Thursday evening, Neil hoped he'd be able to get some serious writing done before the program kicked off. Violet had wanted to arrive the moment they could, and he'd liked the idea of unplugging from the rest of the world to focus on his work. He gave Mimi a nod.

"I'm looking forward to the party. And the program, of course."

"We like to open the cabins a little early, in case our artists need some time to set up their equipment." Mimi's hands moved in arcs through the air. "We want to get started on time."

"Sounds good." He had no major equipment other than his laptop, so he didn't comment on that. "I should get back to the airport van. My daughter's waiting."

"Oh!" She tittered. "Of course, of course. Let me know if you need anything at all."

"I appreciate that. See you later." He nodded and turned to go. Unless he missed his guess, he had about thirty seconds before Violet came looking for him.

"Thanks again for coming!"

The words echoed behind him, and he shot another grin over his shoulder before he exited.

He wasn't sure how he was going to get everything done this summer, and probably should have turned the invitation down. As a bestselling novelist-cum-screenwriter, he'd had non-stop deadlines since he'd signed his first book contract. The ink had barely dried on his college diploma when he'd landed that deal. He'd hit the *New York Times* list with his third novel and, as amazing as that was, it meant he hadn't had a real break in a long, long time.

Not that being an artist-in-residence qualified as a vacation, but Vi had loved the idea and they could use some away time to unwind. Having Vi living with him full-time this year had been a huge adjustment for them both. Since the divorce, she'd spent the school year with her mom in Maine and summers in California with him. His ex-wife, Cara, and he had managed a friendly relationship for their daughter's sake. Losing her had been a blow for him too. He hadn't been in love with her anymore, but they had history, and it was painful to see someone who'd once meant the world to him gone too young, too soon.

Yeah, he could use a respite and so could Vi, preferably somewhere they'd never been before. Better still, somewhere Cara had never been, somewhere with no memories. That was why, despite being behind on his latest book deadline and owing screenplay adaptations on four of his novels to a film company, he'd agreed to this residency. Of course, he'd had to swear to his publisher and the film company that he'd have his book and a draft of the first script done by the end of the summer program in order for them not to freak the hell out.

Even if it meant he'd be mentoring a new writer along the way—adding to his already overflowing plate—if this trip made his too-somber daughter happy, he'd find a way to work it all out.

It was that simple, and that difficult.

"Did you get the keys?" As suspected, Violet was crawling out of the van.

"Yep." He shook the envelope, which jangled metallically. Shooing her back with his free hand, he resumed his seat.

"There's a sign with arrows." Vi pointed before snapping on her seatbelt. "We're that way. Cabin 3B."

"Got it." The driver glanced in the rearview mirror for a moment, then signaled and turned right, heading toward a long line of small buildings.

They pulled up to the specified cabin a minute later, and Vi was out of the vehicle in under three seconds. She sprinted up the stairs and flew through the door. Neil unfolded himself from the van slowly, still feeling every single kink in his muscles. After lacing his fingers together, he lifted his arms overhead and stretched from head to toe. More than a few joints gave satisfying pops.

The driver heaved their suitcases out onto a grassy path beside the dirt road, and Neil tipped him generously. With a silent nod, the other man disappeared, and the van pulled away.

After picking up two of the three bags, Neil followed his daughter inside.

"Wow, this is teeny."

"Mmm." He made the sound as noncommittal as possible.

The place lacked square footage but was still one of the more spacious cabins available. A quick walk-through showed it had a living room, a miniscule bathroom, and two small bedrooms. No kitchen. The briefing packet he'd received had warned that there was electricity, but no Wi-Fi internet, and they were way outside of cell phone range. *Thank God.* If anyone wanted to get in touch, they had to call and leave a message with the main lodge. The lodge had a computer they could check emails on once a day. Twenty minutes per day, max, and the connection was dialup.

Perfect.

He'd never have guessed he'd be excited to disconnect, but it just showed him how much he'd needed this trip for himself. Not just to make Vi happy.

"Looks like I get the room that's tinier than your walk-in closet in LA. Cozy." She passed him to flop onto the single bed, apparently claiming her territory.

"There are only two other families here with kids, so we get the deluxe editions. Some of the cabins are studios—no separate bedroom."

Her dark brows winged up. "Any kids my age?"

"Not sure." He propped his shoulder against the doorjamb. "Guess we'll find out at breakfast tomorrow."

"That's right. Cafeteria-style eating, like at school. And we have to play lunch ladies twice a week." Her expression was a cross between fascinated and horrified by the prospect of cooking for dozens of artists.

He grinned. "There will be other folks helping us, but yes."

"That also means five days a week, people need to wait on me." She folded her hands behind her head, looking pleased. "I like that."

"You realize we have a housekeeper who waits on you seven days a week at home, right?"

She made a face at him, and he reached over to ruffle her curls. She jerked upright. "Hey, now! Not the hair."

It was weird that she suddenly cared about her hair. She'd also started playing with makeup. He wouldn't allow anything too crazy, but she was in junior high, so he understood it was a losing battle. He sighed and hoped like hell if any of the other kids here were her age, none of them were cute boys. He wasn't sure he was ready to handle her first major crush.

"I'm going to grab the last suitcase." She hopped up and jogged outside.

He called after her, "Call me if it's too heavy."

"KK!"

"You could just say okay. I don't need two Ks!"

"OMG, Daaaaaaaad!" The wail was just satisfying enough to make him grin and recall how much his parents had bugged him for using slang as a teen. The cycle came full circle.

The cabin was a bit stuffy, so he walked around and opened all the windows. The sun was starting to dip behind the mountains, and the sky was streaked with shades of orange and gold, pink and purple. It was gorgeous. He stood there for a moment, taking deep breaths and trying to let all his stress go.

Then he heard the sound of his daughter's voice, talking to someone else. So he headed outside to see what was up. A woman stood chatting with Vi, and it was clear his daughter hadn't so much as touched the suitcase yet.

But it was the woman who caught his eye. She had her back to him, so all he could see was that she had vivid teal streaks in her dark hair, a petite build, and an ass perfect enough to make any heterosexual man drool.

"Hey, Dad! Come meet our new neighbor. She's in 3A. It's one of the studios, but she says it's bigger than the flat she had in London and has a better view."

The woman chuckled and moved aside to make room for him. "I loved that flat, but it did have its drawbacks."

She had an American accent, so she wasn't English, but that was all he could tell about her. Her dark eyes were wide and lovely and a little mysterious, like she knew many secrets and relished every single one of them. The sudden need to touch her gripped him, so he was glad he could offer a hand to shake. It was nice when social norms coincided with physical wants. "Hi. I'm Neil Graves. And you are...?"

She took it, her grip firm. Then she blinked at him. "Neil Graves, the horror writer?"

"One and the same." A buzz of awareness sizzled up his arm, goose bumps breaking over his flesh. Heat flashed like lightning within him, and he wanted her. No questions, no wondering why. It was simply fact. He pulled his hand back because they weren't alone, and now wasn't the time to hit on someone he'd only just met.

But she could tell—that same awareness sparked in her gaze. The smile she offered him was more than a little impish. This lady had the kind of charisma that drew people in like a Lorelei. She wasn't the most beautiful woman he'd ever seen—he'd had too many years around the physical perfection of Hollywood starlets—but she had skin as smooth as alabaster, high cheekbones, and a generous mouth that made him think of things he really shouldn't. His body began to stir with interest.

Down boy.

Dear God. Please, please don't let this woman be the author he was supposed to mentor. He'd spend the summer with a semi, wishing his khakis were a whole lot looser.

He tried to keep his voice even. "So are you a mentor or mentee for the program?"

"Mentor."

Thank you, sweet baby Jesus. His smile probably reflected far too much relief. "That's great!"

Brow furrowed in confusion, she tilted her head, and the fading sun caught on her jewelry. She had a tiny diamond stud in her nose, two delicate gold earrings in each lobe, and an electric blue metal hoop in her tragus. A wicked part of him wondered if she might have more intimate parts of her body pierced too. He gave himself a mental shake. That was the last thing he should be thinking about anyone at The Enclave—he had many more important things that should be on his mind. Like his daughter and his deadlines and his mentee. Yep, he was busy.

He hoped he didn't run into his neighbor too often, because he sincerely doubted his libido would be up to resisting this unexpected and unwanted attraction. He hadn't felt this sudden burn of need for a woman in more years than he could remember, and it was damn inconvenient for it to happen now.

He cleared his throat. "My protégé is an aspiring novelist, though I'm masquerading as a screenwriter this summer."

That charming smile returned full force. "The movie sequel to *Dead and Gone*? Nice. I liked the first film, and the books are even better."

"Thanks." He rubbed a hand over the back of his neck, feeling inordinately flattered. It wasn't as if he'd never been complimented on his work before.

The corners of her eyes crinkled. "I read your books when I go visit my parents, just to remind myself that it could be worse. Someone could be giving me a machete mani-pedi. That would be mildly more painful, and it's good to keep that in mind."

"I'm glad I could help." He kept his tone even, uncertain if he should laugh or not. "Uh...what kind of artist are you?"

"Painter. I'm Laurel Pa—"

Violet broke in, "Hey, Dad! I can't lift the suitcase with your fifty tons of research books."

He turned to his daughter. When had she moved? He would swear she'd been standing next to him the whole time. One more reason to stay away from the neighbor—she was hell on his focus. "That's my cue. Gotta go. It was interesting to meet you."

Interesting. Great. That was what guys said to suspected axe-murderers while they sidled away, hoping not to get impaled in the back when they turned to run like hell. Laurel's flirting skills were seriously rusty if she couldn't manage a few sentences with a hot guy before he bolted.

Ah, well. She wasn't here to flirt. She was here to get her creativity on.

With a last glance at the adorable teen girl and her tall, dark, handsome, and—as Violet had so helpfully mentioned—divorced dad, Laurel turned to jog back over to her little cabin in the woods. She had some unpacking to do, and she wanted to get her sketchbook out so she had it on hand when the sun rose in the morning. She had a feeling the view was going to be inspiring.

It took about ten minutes to unearth her sketchpad because she had to wade through the crates of canvases, paints, and other supplies she'd had to ship ahead. Tomorrow would need to include a major unpack-a-thon.

Loud knocking meant she had to play a game of hopscotch across the cabin. "One second!"

Jerking the door open brought her face-to-fist with Neil. He dropped his hand. "Hi, again. Would you mind—?"

"I can't wait." Violet darted around them and pelted toward the bathroom. "Our toilet's broken. Need to pee."

The door slammed shut.

Laurel turned back to Neil. "Did you turn the toilet on?"

His forehead puckered, bafflement on his face. "Turn it on?"

Oh, she couldn't resist. "Yes, like with a woman. Turning on is an important part of the process."

Instead of being offended, he went from being merely good-looking to being full-on attractive when he snorted out a laugh. "Okay, how do I turn on the toilet?"

"The directions are in the envelope with the keys." She shot a sympathetic glance in the direction of the bathroom. "Though if you didn't use the restroom in the lodge before you got to the cabin, I can imagine you just needed to take a leak and didn't bother looking for special toilet instructions."

He nodded. "It was a long drive from Denver."

"Basically, they shut the water off to the toilets when the cabins aren't in use. You have to twist the knobby thing to turn it back on."

"Knobby thing, huh?" He forked a hand through his shoulder-length dark hair as his brows winged upward, a tiny smile playing at his lips. Damn, he had a dimple in his left cheek. He had rugged good looks, angular features, and a few brackets around his eyes and mouth. It was entirely unfair that those kinds of lines made a man more distinguished, but made a woman appear haggard. Laurel got to enjoy a nice view though, so she wasn't going to protest.

He propped an arm on the doorjamb, and she angled herself a bit closer. If she wasn't mistaken, that was pure male interest flashing in his gray eyes. A frisson of desire skipped over her skin, hot and sweet. It had been far too long since she'd been this drawn to a guy, and she liked it.

"Yeah, knobby thing. It's a technical term." She bit her lower lip and his gaze dropped to her mouth.

"Very technical." He leaned forward a little, and for a split second, she thought he might kiss her. Her breath caught, anticipation humming through her. She tipped her head back a bit, an invitation. She really wouldn't mind knowing if he tasted as good as he looked. His pupils expanded, lust flushing his face.

Well, hot damn. Her flirting skills seemed to be resurfacing. Though maybe they could have picked a better time than when they were discussing toilets.

As if on cue, Violet flushed loudly. A few seconds later, there came the sound of running water.

The mood broken, Neil eyed her thoughtfully. "You know, Laurel, I didn't catch your last name earlier."

The bathroom door opened, and Violet's popped her head out. "She's Laurel Patton, Dad. She's, like, kind of famous."

Neil and Laurel jerked away from each other, as if the teen had caught them doing something naughty. Laurel almost wished they had been, even though having anyone walk in on an intimate moment was beyond awkward. But utter want still pulsed through her, a need that was entirely unfulfilled.

Her laugh was breathy when she met his gaze. "Only famous in my own little art bubble. You're pretty well-known by the general population."

He inclined his head. "The hazard of having your book series turned into films."

"Starring the hottest actor on the planet," Laurel couldn't help but point out.

"It doesn't hurt, no." His gaze was intent on her face, and it felt as if he could see straight to her soul. The pure, piercing silver of his eyes was a little uncanny.

"Right." She tucked a lock of hair behind her ear, uncharacteristically flustered. It wasn't as if she'd never been attracted to anyone before. Jesus, she needed to get a grip.

Violet grinned at her. "I saw one of your shows in New York with my mom a couple years ago. You had bangs then, and they were purple."

"Ha, yes, the purple. I know which show that was, then." Laurel clasped her hands behind her back and rocked up onto her toes. "You've got a good memory."

"Thanks." The teen beamed at the compliment, and Laurel had a feeling she'd just won a fangirl for the summer.

"What did you think of the show?"

"It was cool." But something in her expression dimmed. "Mom wanted to buy one of your paintings, but the one she liked best had already been sold."

Laurel shrugged sympathetically. "That's the problem with one-of-a-kind art pieces."

"Books are a lot easier that way," Neil broke in, the skin around his eyes tightening with...worry? "Everyone who wants to buy a copy can."

"True." Laurel glanced back and forth between father and daughter. The mood had shifted, but she couldn't put her finger on how or why. Maybe something to do with Neil's divorce from Violet's mother? She couldn't tell, but the strain was obvious. Laurel tried for a brighter tone. "Well, I should have several new pieces done by the end of the residency. Maybe your mom can take a look and see if she likes any of them."

Violet's countenance went from dim to bleak. "My mom died last year."

Heart clenching so tight it was hard to breathe, Laurel reached out to squeeze the teen's shoulder. "Oh, damn, sweetie. That's a rough thing to deal with."

A little chortling snort escaped the girl, and she swiped quickly at her eyes. "Thanks for not saying *I'm sorry*. I hate when people do that. They didn't even know her, so they're not really sorry."

"You're right." Laurel nodded, glad she hadn't made the situation worse with her blunt condolences. "It's just some empty thing people say when they don't know what else to say."

"Yeah." Violet's chin set mulishly. "It's stupid."

"Sadly, there's a lot of stupid in the world." Laurel heaved a mournful sigh, hoping it was dramatic enough to make the teen smile.

She got a wrinkled nose and another snort. She'd take that.

"We should probably head back and unpack." Neil reached out and pulled his daughter in close. It wasn't quite a hug, but the gesture of support wouldn't make the girl feel babyish. Nicely done. Another mark in Neil Graves's favor.

"It's gotten dark." Laurel turned and pulled out one of the flashlights she'd found in the table by the door. "Take this."

"Good thinking." Violet snagged it, flicked it on, and turned for the porch steps. "And I'm so glad your bathroom was working."

"Happy to be of assistance. See you later!"

Neil looked at Laurel for a few seconds, his gaze again intent and incisive. His expression was unreadable, but he mouthed "thank you" before he disappeared into the darkness.

After they'd gone, Laurel sagged against the wall. Violet was a trip—quirky and bright and handling a terrible loss with a grace that people three times her age couldn't manage. Neil was...intense. It was the only word she could use to describe him. He was nothing like the light and easy men she was usually attracted to, and she wasn't sure if that was a good thing or not. As if she had a say in the matter. A reluctant grin tugged at her lips. She had to admit she liked the way it felt when he looked at her with attraction burning in his gaze, and she definitely wanted more of that. How much more and how far she'd let this go emotionally, she didn't yet know but couldn't wait to find out.

One thing was certain: this was going to be a summer to remember.

CHAPTER THREE

L aurel didn't sleep very well that night. After years in city apartments, it was weird trying to sleep without cars and buses rolling by all night. There were no streetlights to shine through her windows, no cheerful drunks singing on the sidewalk, no alley cats hissing and fighting. At first she thought it was weirdly silent, but then she heard owls hooting, wind rippling through tree leaves, the occasional crunch of footsteps as someone walked along the dirt road outside. The sounds were different than what she was used to, and it took a long time to drop into slumber.

That meant she really needed coffee the next morning. Only there was no coffee in her cabin. No, she had to walk all the way over to the lodge to get her caffeine fix. She stumbled through a shower and getting dressed, then did a zombie-like walk up the road to the main building.

Breakfasts were self-serve cold cereal, pastries, bagels, and fruit. Everyone was in charge of clearing their own messes in the mornings.

Which meant, thankfully, that none of the handful of people that had already arrived tried to speak to her before she'd had some coffee. She hunkered down at a table in the corner with a croissant and two ceramic mugs full of liquid ambrosia. Yes, she was double-fisting her caffeine. No, she was not ashamed.

It took both cups and another fifteen minutes of staring into space before she started to feel normal. She glanced around, but didn't recognize anyone. She didn't see her new neighbors, and she had to admit she was a little disappointed. Which was silly because she'd spent a grand total of maybe thirty minutes with them. Still, she would have liked to run into them, but they definitely weren't among those sitting in the large dining room.

As if her thoughts had conjured them, Neil and Violet walked in the door. He was dressed in khakis and a T-shirt that hugged his broad shoulders—*oh, yum*—while his daughter looked as if she'd just rolled out of bed. She wore a pair of mesh basketball shorts, a wrinkled tank top, and her dark hair stood up in odd clumps and flyaway wisps. They grabbed trays of food, and the teen's face creased in a grin when she spotted Laurel. Waving them over, Laurel tidied up her dirty dishes to make room.

"Morning," Violet said, the word almost swallowed by her enormous yawn. She parked herself next to Laurel, leaving Neil a seat across from them. He had a book tucked under his arm, and he set it next to his tray.

After Vi yawned again, Laurel laughed. "You look lively."

"Not a morning person." The teen shoveled in an enormous bite of Cheerios. "Never have been."

"She's not lying." Neil stirred sugar into his black coffee. "Vi was the only baby in history to sleep in from the day she was born. We had to wake her up on Christmas mornings."

"Lucky dog. My nephew Nick has been up before sunrise every day of his life. I'm fairly certain my brother and sister-in-law would kill for the chance to sleep in." Laurel widened her eyes. "I know I would when I'm on overnight babysitting duty."

"You have a brother?" There was just a hint of wistfulness to Violet's question.

Neil tensed, and his face went blank, but he said nothing. Hmm, so siblings were a sore subject, huh? Did he have one he hated, or did Violet want a baby brother or sister and never got one?

"Yep. Tate's two-and-a-half years older than me. He's the most amazing big bro of all time." Laurel cast a conspiratorially wink at the girl. "Don't tell him I said so."

"I won't. It's cool you have a sibling though. I'm the only child of only children. I don't even have any cousins."

Going with the topic Neil clearly had no control over, Laurel looked at him askance and pressed a hand between her breasts. "No cousins? How could you deprive your daughter this way?"

"I'm a terrible human being, clearly," he replied, sotto voce. His gaze dropped for a split-second to her chest before he focused on his coffee. "I was involved in a multigenerational scheme to make my kid miserable. That's what fathers live for, isn't it?"

"Especially fathers of teen girls." Laurel added sagely, "It's a scientific fact."

He snorted and cracked a grin. Somehow that felt like a victory, considering his face seemed to be perpetually sober. She wondered when the last time was that he laughed until he cried, or if he'd ever smiled so broadly his cheeks hurt. It had probably been a long time—those brackets around his eyes weren't laugh lines.

Laurel nudged Vi's shoulder. "Look on the bright side. No nephew will ever wake you up screaming at four AM."

"Dad's the one up at the crack of dawn." Violet shook her head as if the concept was beyond comprehension.

"It means I make it to breakfast showered and dressed." He cast a glance at her wild hair.

Laurel reached over to lift a particularly woolly bit of the teen's coif. "And he can prove he knows how to use this magical device called a brush."

Bursting into laughter, she swatted at Laurel's hand.

"I'm just a nice daughter who, like, let you and Mom write in the mornings before I bugged you for food." Her smile was sunny and just a touch benevolent. "You're welcome."

He harrumphed and slathered cream cheese on his bagel. Laurel smothered a chuckle, and he cast her a glance full of rueful humor. A kick of attraction hit her again, the longing so sharp and insistent, she had to look away.

"You gave your mom writing time too? She was an author?" Laurel thought she vaguely remembered that being mentioned in some news article she'd read about Neil when his last book series was announced. She didn't recall much else—she'd only been looking for release dates. Though she might have to Google him now. Perhaps that was cheating, but she didn't care.

"Mom wrote as Cara O'Neil." The teen drew up a knee and rested it against the edge of the table. She picked up a triangle of toast and munched on it. "But I—"

"Wait, wait." Laurel held up a hand. "Your parents are the warm-fuzzy hometown romance author and the king of blood-curdling psycho-thrillers?"

Vi nodded, her expression turning woeful. "I'm going to need so much therapy."

Man, she adored this kid. A belly laugh escaped Laurel. "Yeah, that's a recipe for warped."

"Hey, now," Neil protested. He opened the book he'd brought, scanning through what appeared to be the table of contents. "We gave you a well-balanced appreciation of genre literature. You're welcome, ingrate."

"What are you looking up?" his daughter asked.

"Fact-checking something for *Dead Fall*." He flipped to a chapter in the middle. "I need to know how quickly a person bleeds out if you sever their carotid artery with a ski pole."

Laurel sat back in her chair. "Yeah, that's the definition of well-adjusted and balanced."

"I do what I can." He chuckled quietly, meeting her eyes again as he rose to his feet. "Though I'm better adjusted with copious amounts of coffee. Excuse me."

Forcing herself not to stare at his ass as he walked away, she turned back to Violet. "You know, I've read a few Cara O'Neil books."

"A lot of people did. She sold really well." The girl's expression was both proud and sad. "Though I think she was kinda bummed she'd used Dad's name as part of her pen name, after the divorce and everything."

"I could see that. I'm kinda bummed my real last name is attached to my dad. He's an ass."

"My dad's cool." She straightened. "I'm gonna use O'Neil as my pen name too. As a reminder of both my parents. I'm writing a book this summer too."

Her declaration was almost defiant, as if someone had told her she couldn't possibly write a book. Laurel had trouble imagining that person was Neil. Maybe a friend? Kids had such a heavy influence on each other. She doubted that had changed much since she was in middle school.

"Oh, yeah? That's pretty cool. I had no idea what I wanted to do with my life when I was your age."

"Well, if both my parents were authors…" Vi took a big bite of toast, then shoved it to the side of her mouth and spoke through her food. "Then it's genetic."

"Absolutely part of your DNA," Laurel agreed. How her parents might explain her artistic career, she wasn't sure. Genetic anomaly? Genetic defect? Yeah, probably a defect.

"It's going to be young adult mystery, but my heroine totally gets the hottie in the end."

"So a little bit of both your parents again?"

Vi's eyes—the same silvery gray as her father's—narrowed in consideration. "Yeah, kinda. Though my mom only wrote about girls getting with guys, and I haven't decided yet if the hottie my heroine gets is a guy or a girl."

"There's nothing wrong with the sapphic route." Laurel had never met a teenager quite like Violet. In just the day she'd known her, the girl had proven to be smart, funny, and strong. Also, a little nutty, which meant it was somehow completely believable that she was not only going to write a novel, but it'd be good enough that she'd need a pen name ready for when it was published. "I can't wait to read it."

"You could, like, beta read what I've written so far." Violet's grin was brilliant. "I have a few chapters."

"I would love to." Hey, Laurel liked a good mystery, and she had no problem with the heroine getting a hottie of any gender at the end of a book. Sounded like a fun story.

"You're gonna love my heroine. She the GOAT."

"She's a goat? Is this a fantasy mystery with a faun?" Laurel felt her face scrunch in confusion.

"Not goat like the animal." Violet seemed delighted to know something Laurel didn't. "It means Greatest Of All Time. GOAT."

"Teenager—it's a whole different language." Neil returned with his coffee, clearly overhearing the last part. "I could make another fortune writing a Teen-English dictionary for parents."

"It would change too fast." Vi appeared dubious. "It's not like we say the same thing all the time."

"GOAT. I'll remember that," Laurel promised.

The three of them finished up their meals, and then Neil pushed back from the table. "I'm going to see if I can use the business center for a few minutes, check email, and print some documents. Did you want to come with me, Vi, or head back to the cabin by yourself?"

"Cabin. I need to shower." Vi poked Laurel's arm. "And use the magic brush."

Keeping her voice as serious as possible, Laurel said, "I hear they work wonders, those magic brushes."

"Haha." The teen stuck out her tongue, chugged her orange juice, and then carted her tray off to the clean-up area.

When Laurel turned back it was to find Neil's assessing gaze pinning her in place. He had the kind of look that said she was some sort of odd creature he couldn't quite figure out. She stiffened in reflex, far too used to a similar look from her parents. Her chin jutted and she folded her arms.

His eyebrows arched, but he didn't comment on her defensive posture. "You're really good with Violet. She's not normally this friendly with people she's just met."

Well. That wasn't what she'd been expecting. A lopsided grin formed on her mouth. "I have that effect on some people."

"You definitely have an effect on people," he murmured. His expression went roguish, but he turned away before she could come up with a witty reply.

Maybe her flirting skills were even rustier than she'd suspected.

Well, she could practice more on Neil later. Practice made perfect, right? She picked up her tray and walked over to drop it and her dishes off. All right, then. Time to start the day.

She had one thing on her agenda that she needed to handle before she went back to her cabin to organize all her stuff. Being part of The Creative Enclave—whether you were an artist-in-residence or an aspiring artist—meant that you had to help in the communal kitchen. Everyone had to cook, clean, and serve the buffet style meals twice a week. Once for lunch and once for dinner.

She wanted introduce herself to the chef. She had the first lunch shift on Monday, so it was best to find the person who'd make sure she didn't give anyone food poisoning. Cooking wasn't Laurel's strong suit. She hadn't killed anyone yet, but no one ever asked her for recipes either. Her idea of entertaining involved a nice bottle of wine and some really good cheese. Hey, it worked for her.

Slipping into the kitchen, she took in the gleaming stainless steel prep surfaces and industrial grade appliances. At a massive cutting board stood an imposing woman who was as round as she was tall, with scraped back salt-and-pepper hair, and smooth dark brown skin that belied the gray bun. She turned to level a gimlet eye on Laurel, clearly establishing dominance. The look said, *don't mess with me—I will kill you.*

"What do you want?" she barked.

Laurel snapped to attention. "Hi, I'm Laurel Patton. I'm supposed to help make lunch on Monday."

"Gloria," the woman grunted in return, slamming a meat cleaver through a slab of beef. "I run the kitchen here. You one of those artsy fartsy people?"

"Yep."

Stabbing the cleaver in Laurel's direction, Gloria said, "I don't give a damn how famous you are, you hear me? When you're in my kitchen, you do as I say."

"Yes, ma'am," Laurel drawled, fighting a smile. She couldn't help it; the situation struck her as funny all of the sudden.

The older woman's eyes narrowed to dangerous slits. "I own many knives."

"And know how to use them. I'm suitably intimidated." Laurel gave up the struggle, offering a full-blown grin. She'd come here so excited to be respected—maybe slightly revered—for her craft and one of the first people she ran into didn't give a flying rat's ass. Ah, irony. "How about you just boss me around, and I let you, and we pretend you're not tempted to carve me up for the soup pot?"

Gloria harrumphed. "I'll consider it."

"Thank you." Laurel injected as much humble sincerity as possible into her tone.

"Grandma!" A girl wearing a Seattle Storm T-shirt and basketball shorts came rocketing through the door, skidding to a stop in front of Gloria.

"Ruth, I have told you not to run in my kitchen. I've got hot pots and sharp utensils in here. You could get hurt, and then I'll never hear the end of it from your mother and father. Which means you'll never hear the end of it from me."

"Sorry, Grandma." A puckish grin lit the kid's face, showing off deep dimples. She looked about twelve years old, still all awkward knees and elbows, but with feminine curves starting to form. She had the smooth complexion of her grandmother, though several shades darker, with a riot of springy ebony curls, and luminous black eyes. With that mischievous smile and gorgeous bone structure, the girl was going to be a knockout in a couple of years. Laurel didn't envy her parents when the female-attracted half of the teen population started banging down the door.

Gloria heaved a sigh. "Child, you're going to be the death of me."

"I love you." Ruth threw her arms around her grandmother's thick middle.

"I love you too." The older woman's voice went from indulgent to stern in the blink of an eye. "Now go play. Do not run indoors."

"'Kay!" Ruth pirouetted, then strolled out of the room. As soon as she rounded the corner, the sound of her footsteps increased until she was clearly pelting across the lodge at top speed.

Shaking her head, Gloria sighed again, but then slanted a disgruntled glance at Laurel. "Her parents are off on a second honeymoon, so Ruthie's spending her summer vacation with me."

"She's adorable." Laurel didn't have to feign her sincerity.

"Got me wrapped around her pinkie." Gloria slid a fingertip along the edge of a wicked-sharp butcher knife lying on her cutting board. "Don't think I'm that lenient with anyone but her."

Keeping her expression suitably solemn, Laurel nodded. "I was under no such illusions."

"Good. You're not an idiot. Now, go away." The older lady flicked her cleaver in a dismissive gesture. "I don't need you here for another couple of days."

"Yes, ma'am." With that, Laurel executed a quick about-face and escaped while she still could.

Once she'd gotten outside—safely beyond Gloria's hearing—she leaned back against the wall and laughed her ass off.

D amn, she was beautiful.

The thought slammed into Neil as he walked up to the lodge, and the sound of her laughter lilted on the breeze. He'd gotten halfway to his cabin and realized he'd forgotten to pick up his paperwork from the printer, so he'd had to come back. Now, he mounted the porch stairs and the sight of her stopped him in his tracks. Last night, he'd thought her pretty, but her laugh, her pure joy, made her exquisite, breathtaking.

It was a dual punch to the chest and groin when she looked up and met his gaze. The mirth faded from her expression, and pure electric attraction sparked between them. His heart thudded against his ribs. Her tongue flicked out to slide along her lower lip, and his shaft went rock hard.

Bam, zero to horny in two-point-five seconds.

It was starting to become his automatic response any time she was nearby.

Her voice was low and smoky when she spoke. "Neil."

"Laurel." He took the last step up, joining her on the porch. There was still four feet between them, but he felt a magnetic draw toward her. He knew almost nothing about her, but suddenly he wanted to. He shouldn't, because he suspected knowing more would make him desire her more, but he'd rarely experienced this instantaneous burn of craving for a woman, and never this intensely.

Added to that, she'd dealt with Violet and the awkward mom-just-died moment in a way that actually made his daughter laugh. That never happened. He wouldn't have guessed it was possible. He'd tried to thank her last night, but there'd been no real way to do that without turning it into the awkward situation he was glad they'd avoided.

Then this morning, she'd gotten Violet to speak in coherent sentences before nine AM. It bordered on miraculous.

Everything about Laurel seemed designed to pique his interest.

She took a breath, lifting her breasts, and he couldn't help but enjoy the effect. She wasn't the most endowed woman he'd ever met, but his palms itched to cup the small, pert mounds.

"Honestly, I always thought Graves was a pseudonym to make you sound more horror-y." She squinted and tilted her head. "Horror-ish?"

So far, he hadn't been able to predict what might come out of her mouth, and she'd managed to catch him by surprise again.

"Horror-ish," he replied after a beat of silence, injecting as much certainty into his voice as he could.

Her lips pursed. She sidled to the right, a little closer to him, and stood just in front of the screen door. "You're sure?"

"I am the writer." Now he went for wounded dignity. Yep, he was flirting. No, he really shouldn't, for a million reasons, but she was pretty and funny and fascinating as hell.

"Uh-huh." That thousand-watt smile of hers flashed. "That means you make shit up for a living."

"Absolutely." He winked.

She rocked back on her heels. "I bet Graves made it easy to pick a genre, huh?"

He chuckled and took a step forward. "I never had a publisher ask me to take on a penname, that's for sure."

The pounding of footsteps sounded, and then the door slammed open—right into Laurel's back.

"Sorry!" A piping young voice came from inside. "I need out."

"Whoops!" Laurel hopped forward to let the girl pass, tripped over a porch floorboard, twisted to try to catch herself, but tumbled against him anyway. She hit him hard enough to force a grunt out of him.

On reflex, he snapped his arms around her and they stumbled sideways a few steps. His butt hit the porch railing, stopping their momentum.

"Sorry again! Are you, like, okay and everything?"

"I'm fine," Laurel replied. "Go play like your grandma said, Ruth."

"'Kay...if you're sure...laters!" After another moment's hesitation, Ruth skipped around the corner of the lodge, gone in seconds.

Then he was left with an armful of soft, sexy woman. His body registered that fact before his brain did, and he went rock hard. After a moment of stunned silence, a snort of mirth burst out of her, but she froze when her hip shifted against his groin.

Yep, that's a raging erection, sweetheart.

She wiggled a little, as if to make sure of what she was feeling. He bit back a groan, but her movements did nothing to help the situation. If anything, he grew even harder. Christ, he'd turned into a randy teenager.

Her head tipped back and their gazes collided. An apology was on the tip of his tongue, but the heat in her expression stopped his words. She bit her lip, and her palm settled against his chest. He stared at her lush mouth, wanting to taste her but holding back. They stood there in throbbing silence for long moments, neither moving, neither pushing away. With every breath, the sexual tension between them ratcheted up. His mind told him to let her go because kissing a woman he barely knew was an idiotic idea. His libido didn't give a damn about the details—it just knew that he craved her with a sharp suddenness that was difficult to deny.

"Oh, what the hell?" A grin kicked up the corner of her mouth, she rose onto tiptoe and kissed him.

He'd been so busy battling with himself that she caught him off-guard. She flicked her tongue out, sliding along the seam of his lips.

He groaned and let her in, dueling with her for control of the kiss. This was no tentative seeking, just hot possession. The flavor of her exploded over his taste buds—sweet woman and a hint of coffee. His hands clamped on her hips, turning her so she faced him squarely, and pulled her tight to his body. Their angles and curves fitted beautifully, and his body pulsed with painful need. He let his palms glide up her back, enjoying the resilient warmth of her skin through her T-shirt.

She arched against him, nipping at his upper lip. He jolted at the sensation, pure lust roaring through his veins. His fingers dove down to curl around her backside, the lush curves filling his hands. So fucking perfect. His breathing sped to ragged gasps, and little mewls broke from her throat. Dear God, she was like pure fire twisting in his arms. He slid his thigh between hers, pulling her tighter against him. She moved on him, grinding down on his leg. He could feel the heat of her through his khakis and her shorts, and it was almost enough to make his skull explode.

One part of him couldn't believe he was dry humping a woman on a porch, where anyone could walk up and see them. Another part of him didn't want to let her go. Not yet. He mated his tongue with hers, the rhythm matching the thrust and slide of their hips. The friction was too good, too much, and he was embarrassingly close to coming in his pants. When her fingertips circled his nipple, then tweaked the tip, he had to pull back. Otherwise he was going to drag her to the wood floor and take her then and there.

"That was…" She made a little humming noise. "Awesome."

"I wasn't expecting…" A rough exhalation spilled out of him. He had no idea how to finish that sentence without insulting her or looking like an utter fool.

"This? Me, neither." She eased out of his arms and forked her fingers through her teal-streaked hair. "I always love a nice surprise.

Don't you?"

"I can't complain." Only a moron would. A kiss that good? Damn. Then again, that hadn't been just a kiss, had it? He'd been a half-second away from fucking her. Just thinking about it made his still-hard erection pulse.

She opened her mouth to speak, but Violet's voice cut through their conversation.

"Hey, Dad! I just met the chef's granddaughter. She's here all summer too." Violet mounted the stairs, the same girl who'd slammed into Laurel right on Vi's heels. "This is Ruth."

"We bumped into each other," Laurel replied drily.

"I really am sorry." The younger girl gave a bashful shrug. "I go everywhere at a run. My dad says I need to, like, join the track and field team when I start middle school next year."

"That's awesome." Vi shrugged. "I'm so not sporty at all."

"You don't have to run with me." Ruth's midnight eyes twinkled good-naturedly. "Want me to show you the lake? Did you bring your bathing suit?"

"Yes and yes." Violet brightened. "I love swimming."

"Sweet. Go change and I'll meet you back here. Ten minutes?"

She turned to Neil. "Is that cool, Dad?"

"Sure." It had been a long time since his daughter had done anything spontaneous. Even this residency had been researched to death. Ruth might be a wrecking ball on two legs, but she seemed to tempt Vi into throwing caution aside. He resisted the urge to ask questions about lifeguards or insist on promises to be careful. It was Violet—she'd be far more careful than he would have at her age. "Be in the dining room at noon for lunch."

"KK!"

He waved them off, and the girls headed in different directions.

And that left him alone with Laurel. Should he bring up the kiss again? Let it go and chalk it up to momentary insanity? He knew the second option was the best one, but he didn't like it. Still, he was an adult and he had responsibilities. Making out with a pretty woman wasn't on his to-do list. Though he really wished it was. It sounded a hell of a lot more fun than editing a manuscript.

He swallowed. "I...uh...left some paperwork in the business center."

After a moment of silence, she shook herself. "Oh. Okay."

There was a hint of disappointment to her words, but her expression was difficult to read. A stab of guilt hit him. He was being an ass, acting as if that crazy kiss hadn't happened. It wasn't her fault he couldn't figure out if he was coming or going any time she was near. He opened his mouth to say something, but she quickly descended the porch stairs.

"I'll see you around, Graves." She paused to glance back at him. "If you decide you want to spend the next few hours necking while the kids are occupied, I'll be sitting under the tree behind my cabin, sketching the scenery. I wouldn't mind the right kind of interruption."

And the erection that had begun to subside went from semi to full-blown at the mere mention of getting his hands on her again. A shudder ran through him. "I'm not sure a few hours would be enough for what I have in mind."

A flush highlighted her cheekbones. "Tease."

"Not teasing, just honesty." He blew out a breath. "More honesty...I need to use every free second I have on finishing my writing projects. I have a book that's overdue to my editor."

Eyes narrowing, she looked him over. "Am I wrong in assuming you stayed up late last night working? And then got up early this morning?"

"Do I look a little rough around the edges?" He scrubbed a hand over his unshaven chin. He'd bathed but hadn't taken the time to shave. He could see the evidence of it along her chin and jaw, a bit of redness. He liked seeing his mark on her way more than he should.

"No, but I don't mind a little roughness in a man." Her tone was innocent, but her expression was sinful enough to make his body throb.

A million ideas flowed through his mind about what she might consider a little rough. At this rate, he'd be taking a cold shower instead of writing.

She made a shooing motion. "Go write, Graves. I'll catch you later."

"I might not be that hard to catch." Now why had he said that? Clearly, he was an idiot. There was no other rational explanation.

A laugh spurted out of her. "I don't mind an easy man either. I'll take a rain check."

With a saucy wink, she strode off, a swing in her hips that made him stare at her ass far too long before he went inside to get his print-outs.

He made it back to his cabin and then stood in the middle of the living room, feeling as if the walls were closing in, staring at his laptop. He'd swear the damn thing was glaring at him, taunting him with the crush of deadlines that were threatening to strangle the life out of him. He knew this feeling, knew that writing today would be a struggle, that he'd fight for every single word. He'd made great strides last night and this morning, but he'd wanted more.

"Damn," he groaned.

After dropping the sheaf of papers on the coffee table, he went to the bedroom to change into a baggy pair of cargo shorts and grab a notepad and pen. He left a quick note for Vi in case she came back from swimming and wanted to know where he was, and then he pushed out the screen door to walk toward the big tree behind Laurel's cabin. Yeah, he probably shouldn't, but he didn't feel like wrestling with his book today. But the novel wasn't the only thing he had to work on. Maybe a change of project and a change of scenery would help.

As promised, Laurel was beneath the leafy canopy, sprawled on her stomach on a blanket with a sketchpad. He kicked off his flip-flops and settled next to her, leaning back against the rough trunk.

"Aren't you supposed to be writing?" She didn't even look up as she asked the question. Her fingers flew gracefully over the paper, the mountains in the distance taking shape in her drawing. Even though he'd never seen her paintings, what he could see now left no doubt of her talent.

He fanned the pages of his notebook. "Outlining. I also have to get a solid draft of my script done by the end of summer."

Her brow crinkled and she stopped drawing. Twisting on the blanket, she looked up at him. "If it's based on your book, shouldn't the outline be obvious?"

"I have to decide what to cut and what to keep, what needs to be tweaked to work on-screen, what directions the actors need to get a scene right." Clicking open his pen, he arched an eyebrow.

She inclined her head, conceding the point. "More complicated than it sounds, then?"

How to put this? "It'd be like me saying that you have a photo of a tree, so it should be obvious how to paint it."

"And that's when I'd want to staple things to your forehead."

He dipped one shoulder in a shrug. "I'd deserve it."

"Sorry for the ignorant question." There was no sarcasm in her tone—the apology was sincere.

"You didn't know." He nudged her leg with his toe. "If you ask something like that again…"

"Staple time?" Humor glinted in her dark chocolate gaze.

He angled his jaw. "It's better than a machete manicure."

"Ha, yes." She rolled to her side, propping her head in her palm. "Topic change. Vi asked me to critique her book. I said yes, but realized maybe I should have asked you if you were okay with that."

"I'm okay with it." He didn't need to think about it. From the interactions he'd seen between her and his daughter, he knew she'd be a good person for Violet to get feedback from.

"Good." She nodded. "I was going to feel like an ass if I had to withdraw the offer."

"I don't know if I should ask you to be gentle or honest. It's her first time trying to write anything like this, so I don't want her to be crushed by criticism, but if she's going to really do this, she's going to have to grow a thick hide because not everyone will be kind. Even blunt honesty can hurt. A lot."

"I'll be both." She reached out to pat his ankle. "I've learned how to balance the two with young painters in my art classes. It's a transferable skill."

"Thank you." He let out a breath. "I don't want to see her hurt. It's…been a rough year for her."

She looked at him for a long moment. "For you too, I'm guessing."

"Yeah. For me too." A rough year, but nowhere near the roughest of his life. He'd had one that was so bad even thinking about it made his gut wrench with pain. So he tried not to think about it.

"How are you holding up?" Now her fingers curled around his ankle, giving a comforting squeeze.

It had been a long, long time since anyone had offered him support. Usually people wanted to take, not to give. Something sweet cinched tight in his chest. Sympathy shone on her face, and she waited patiently for an answer to her question. How was he holding up? Could he say he felt like he was drowning without coming across as pathetic? He'd dealt with crazy deadlines before. He'd been juggling the demands of parenthood for going on fourteen years. Shouldn't it be easier by now? He wished it was. "I'm...fine. Or as fine as I can be."

"Liar." The word was soft.

"Yeah." He let his head fall back against the tree. "It's one of those things where if you start talking about it, if you let some of it out, it'll all come pouring out. I just...I don't have time to do that now."

"Fair enough. But you should give yourself that time. If not now, then soon. If you keep shoving emotions down, they fester, the pressure builds and then...boom. Meltdown, ulcers, therapy. You don't want that. For Violet's sake, if not your own."

Ouch. "Point taken."

"Time to work?"

"Yes, please." Anything but talking about all of his problems.

"That's what I thought." She shifted until she was lying flat again and began adding details to her drawing.

He waited for a few minutes to see if she really meant it. There'd been more than one woman in his life who couldn't stop chatting if there was someone nearby to talk to—Cara had been like that, though hardly the sole offender. But Laurel remained intent on her work, only glancing up at the landscape she was sketching.

Okay. Good. A little surprising, but good. He focused on the paper in front of him, twirled his pen between his fingers a few times, then started jotting down thoughts. Anything and everything was fair game at this stage of the process, so he didn't limit himself or try to edit. That part came later. The wind ruffled through his hair and made the leaves rustle overhead, but it barely registered in his consciousness. He sank into the words he wrote, picturing the scenes until they felt almost real enough to touch.

Even then, he was aware of Laurel. Some corner of his mind noted when she sat up and pulled her sketchbook into her lap, when she flipped to a new page to draw something else. The silence between them was companionable, not loaded with resentment because one of them felt ignored. It was unusual, and he had to admit he liked it.

He had no idea how much time passed as he worked, but his hand flew across the page, the words pouring out of him. Ideas piled up, fighting to get out first. His fingers cramped, his shoulders pulling taut, but he ignored the discomfort. He knew the basic premise of the story, but some things would need to be tweaked, changed, and he could see it so clearly. How to preserve the integrity of the narrative, keep the major plot points and twists, but pare down the excess so that it was just the essentials. Not too much detail for people who hadn't read the book, but not so little detail that it pissed off his hardcore fans who knew the novel and wanted a blow-by-blow movie version. This would work. If it fleshed out the way he envisioned it now, he might even be happy with it. But it would be several months before he knew if that vision came to fruition.

"Hey." Laurel's toes slid down his bare calf.

Even that slight touch was enough to send a tremor through him, and goose bumps broke over his skin. A lightning flash of instantaneous need arced through him. He sucked in a breath, his gaze snapping up to meet hers. Desire roughened his voice. "What?"

Her eyebrows arched, but instead of responding to his tone, she cocked her wrist and tapped her watch. "If you want to meet Violet for lunch, we need to start walking to the lodge."

"It's almost noon?" He scrubbed a hand down his face, still feeling as if he were resurfacing from a deep sleep. It wasn't an unusual state after diving headfirst into the creative process, but this time it was more like he was waking from a wet dream.

She nudged him with her foot again. "Time flies when you're in the zone, right?"

"Definitely." He dropped his notepad onto the grass, pushed to his feet, and slowly stretched out all the kinks. He shook out his hands, flexing his fingers.

After flipping her sketchbook closed, she set it aside and moved to grab the edge of the blanket. He slipped on his flip-flops, and then bent to help her. They worked together to fold up the cover, and he tucked it under one arm. Then he reached over to pick up his tablet of paper.

"Are you happy with what you got done?" She slipped on a strappy pair of leather sandals—dyed an electric shade of pink, of course.

"I am." He let a satisfied smile spread across his face. "Are you?"

"Very." She scooped up her sketchbook. "Shall we?"

"Oh, yeah." Because he couldn't help himself, he dropped a light, lingering kiss on her lush mouth, just letting himself savor the sweet flavor of her. She looked delightfully befuddled when he pulled back, and he enjoyed that far too much.

"Mmm." She sucked her lower lip into her mouth, as if to catch a last taste of him. Dark desire wrenched through him at the sight, and he had to force himself to step back.

"After you, sweetheart."

They dropped everything off at their respective cabins, then walked side by side toward the lodge. Her arm brushed his occasionally, and it sent pinpricks of heat over his flesh. She gave him a glance beneath her eyelashes, a hint of wicked invitation in her gaze. He doubted he could resist the temptation much longer. He'd been struggling against the craving for her since the moment he met her, but he was losing that fight. Maybe there'd never been a real fight in the first place. Instead of wishing the need away, he was starting to savor the burn of anticipation.

An affair with her began to feel like a *when* instead of an *if*. There was something about her that drew him like a moth to flame. The attraction was inevitable, but if he let himself get too distracted from his work, he was going to get burned. Another thing to juggle, but one of the most pleasurable of his competing priorities. Because he had no doubt that they'd be good together.

Their hands bumped for maybe the fifteenth time, and he caught her fingers, linking them with his. She squeezed his hand but made no comment. It was surprisingly nice to have her slim palm nestled against his—when was the last time he'd held a woman's hand? Maybe one or two actresses he'd escorted to some movie premiere or other, but that had been so she could show off for the cameras and make reporters speculate if she was dating him, not because they had any real intimacy to their relationship.

"So," she said, interrupting his thoughts.

"So?"

She swiped her thumb along his palm, making him shudder. "How long to do think it'll be before we—"

Breaking off, she let his hand go. Then she waved toward the large log building before them. "There's Vi and Ruth. Right on time."

Okay, then. If they did begin a fling, she didn't want anyone to know. Her actions now told Neil a great deal. He typically didn't bother to hide his affairs—Vi was aware of who he was seeing at any given time, though he didn't go into any details and she rarely spent much time with the women he slept with. Usually, she never met them. That would be unusual with Laurel, but this summer mentoring program was hardly his norm.

He shoved his hands in his pockets. "With my kid, a few minutes early is a little late."

"Oh, yeah?" She pushed back a loose strand of hair that was dancing in the breeze. "What about you?"

"On time is on time for me. Cara always ran late, but she had to get better about it because it stressed Vi out so bad. She's been that way since the moment we taught her to read a clock." He glanced down to see her smile.

"I try to be on time. My dad's in the early-is-late category too." Something darkened in her normally bright expression, and Neil sensed there was trouble in that father-daughter relationship. A shame. His bond with Violet had been one of the most important factors in his life from the day she was born and wrapped him around her little finger. That was how it should be, in his opinion.

Ruth had gone inside by the time they reached the lodge porch. Vi sat on the rail, her bare legs swinging. She'd put a pair of shorts over her bathing suit, and her towel was slung over her shoulder. "Ruth's eating in the kitchen with her grandma. It's supposed to be tomato basil soup, and we get to build our own sandwiches."

"Did your friend tell you that or did you memorize the menu already?" Neil held open the door and the two ladies entered in front of him.

She gave a sheepish shrug. "A little of both."

"That's a useful skill." Laurel shot a grin over her shoulder at Violet. "I never remember that kind of stuff."

"That's okay. I'll remember for you."

The look on Violet's face told him how much she liked Laurel. If he wasn't mistaken, there was some hero-worship girl-crushing going on there. As potential heroines went, he had no problem with his daughter picking Laurel. Better a respected, dedicated painter than some reality show star. Please God, never let his daughter want to emulate the Kardashians. He could handle wild hair colors, but flashing one's ass—literally—on the internet wasn't his idea of admirable behavior.

"Tomato basil soup sounds awesome." Laurel slapped a hand over her grumbling stomach.

"I'm hungry enough that anything sounds good," Neil agreed.

Violet poked her head in the dining room. "I wonder what kind of bread they have for the sandwiches. There's this place called Pete's back home with marbled rye that was so dope."

"In Maine, not LA," he added for Laurel's benefit.

Something in Vi's tone and wording made him frown. Even after visiting every summer since she was seven and living there for a year, she still didn't think of California as home. He didn't know what he could do to change that, because he sensed part of her pain in the last twelve months was feeling displaced, as if she didn't belong anywhere. He'd offered to relocate to Maine when Cara died, even move back into the house that his ex had gotten in the divorce settlement. It would have been weird as hell, but he'd have done it for Violet. She'd said the house and town reminded her too much of her mom and that she'd rather come to California. But the transition had been rough, and still didn't fit perfectly. He'd let it ride, hoping it got easier with time. He was available if she ever wanted to discuss anything, but mostly she talked about missing Cara when she needed to vent, not the lack of belonging.

"Fooooood." Laurel sniffed the air as they joined the short lunch line.

There were definitely more people than had been there that morning though, and Laurel started chatting with everyone in earshot. She introduced their little group, and by the time they'd reached the front, she had all the particulars on every artist there. She was like sunshine, bright and warm.

More than one of the men gave her an interested glance, and Neil couldn't help the possessiveness that ripped through him. He stepped closer to her, a subtle message to other guys. *Mine. Back off.*

Yes, it was he-man and stupid, but now that he'd stopped fighting the fact that this summer wouldn't be all work and no play, he wasn't about to let some other dude swoop in and try to romance her.

"Let's sit here." Vi trotted over to a table by the window and set her tray down.

Neil slipped into the seat across from his daughter, and he was gratified when Laurel chose the seat next to him. Of course, that meant their legs slid together every time they shifted position, and that was a tease that made the anticipation more intense. Especially since, with his daughter there, he could do nothing about the way he burned for the woman sitting beside him. The conversation was mundane, which was somehow...nice, comfortable. They just caught up with each other about their days, chatted about what they'd like to do with the rest of the weekend.

About halfway through the meal, Ruth popped up and slipped into the only empty chair. She looked at Laurel for a long moment. "Do you have any tattoos?"

Laurel's brows rose. "Why would you think that?"

"Grandma said you might. You have neon hair. You have lots of piercings." Ruth shrugged as if that made it a forgone conclusion that someone like Laurel would have ink.

"I died when I saw her turquoise hair," Vi chimed in. "Dead. Literally dead."

"Yeah, her streaks are on fleek." Ruth bobbed her chin in a nod. "But...does she have tattoos?"

Both girls looked at Laurel expectantly, but she shook her head.

"Nope, sorry. Not a single tat."

Ruth looked a little disappointed. "I figured a painter would have cool tattoos. Like, your own painting on your skin."

"That would be kinda awesome," Violet noted.

"Sorry, girls. Never going to happen. I'm a total wimp when it comes to pain."

Neil cocked a brow. "You have a large number of piercings for a pain wimp."

"One needle and momentary pain. I can handle that. But a really amazing tattoo? That's lots of needles for hours and hours and hours." She shuddered, and he was fairly certain she went a little green.

"No pain," he murmured. "I'll keep that in mind."

Her dark gaze gleamed, knowing that he was talking about something else entirely than body art. "You do that."

He was grateful for the cover the table provided because he could imagine a whole host of ways to provide a lot of pleasure and not a hint of pain.

Ruth turned to Violet, apparently bored with the adults and the lack of tats. "You know there's a rec room here in the lodge, right? It's not, like, awesome or anything, but there's a pool table, ping pong, darts, and satellite TV."

Vi glanced at him, and he nodded his permission. Grinning, she swung back to Ruth. "Let's see what's on TV. If it's boring stuff, we can figure out how to play pool."

"Sweet."

With that, he was summarily abandoned. He should probably be peeved or jealous, but this was the happiest Vi had been in months. Whatever made that happen was a good thing, in his book.

But he could now pick up where his covert conversation with Laurel had left off. "I thought you didn't mind rough, Ms. No Pain."

"There's liking a man with some throw down and then there's *Fifty Shades*. I'm into the first one, not the second." She pursed her lips.

"Any man tries to show me his Red Room, and I'm out of there so fast I'll make his head spin."

Yep, he never knew what might come out of her mouth. He really liked that about her. "I don't have a Red Room, or etchings, or anything else weird to show you."

"A likely story." Her look was exaggeratedly suspicious. "No mirrors mounted over your bed?"

"Well, not in the cabin, but back home..."

She swatted his arm. "Oh, please."

"Finish your soup." He winked and tidied up his tray. As much fun as the sexual banter was, it occurred to him he needed to take care of some parental stuff before he indulged in more personal pleasures.

Doing as he bid, she spooned up the last of her lunch and sat back. "So, what are you up to next, Mr. Deadlines? More script drafting?"

"Eventually." He tapped his fingers over the tabletop. "I have a feeling I should meet the chef if her granddaughter and my daughter are going to spend the summer as BFFs. It's good to know what other parents' or guardians' ground rules are, see if you'd be okay with your kid around their family. Stuff like that."

She blinked. "I don't have any children, so I hadn't even thought of that. You're right, of course, but parenthood requires a whole different way of thinking."

Truer words had never been spoken. "The world is a much scarier place when you have kids, because you see all the dangers to them."

"I imagine those dangers look even crazier when you're an expert in horror." She dabbed a napkin over her mouth, and he suspected she hid a grin.

"I do my best not to be too paranoid." He poked her side, making her squeak and jerk away. If they weren't in public, he'd have taken advantage of the physical closeness tickling a woman allowed. He had no doubt where it would lead.

Soon. Very soon.

CHAPTER FOUR

After dinner that evening, Laurel grinned as she stared at the computer screen. Her brother had sent a new family photo. It took almost five minutes for the picture to download over the slow internet connection, but the wait was worth it. Her nephew was making such a classic grumpy toddler face that she couldn't hold back a laugh. God, she adored that kid. She didn't get to see him often enough. Then again, who did she have to blame for that? No one was keeping her away except herself.

Maybe that was part of the malcontent she'd been feeling before she'd arrived in Colorado. The carefree, rootless lifestyle might be starting to wear on her. Sure, she kept an apartment in San Francisco, and the city wasn't terribly far from her brother, but she had to be in her apartment for the short distance to matter. But she was as likely to be in Paris, Sydney, Cape Town, New York, Tokyo, or some other city anywhere in the world. At first, it had been a way to avoid her parents nagging her to pursue a real job or marry the kind of man who could keep her in paints for the rest of her life. But then it became her habit. She'd been flitting here and there for so long she'd forgotten what it was like have a home.

What she could or should do to change that, she didn't know.

"Hey. You."

Laurel startled at the sound of Gloria's voice behind her. She swiveled in her seat to look at the older woman. "Yes?"

"That boy forgot his hoodie," Gloria groused from where she stood in the business center's doorway. "I don't have time to track people down when they leave things in my dining room."

Since there had been several men of various ages in the dining room today, Laurel had no clue who she was talking about. "Which boy?"

"The one you're hoping to sleep with," Gloria retorted, shoving Neil's offending garment in Laurel's direction. "Why else would I bother telling you about it? Take him the sweatshirt."

Batting her eyelashes, Laurel took the hoodie. "You're a nice lady, Gloria. Trying to help me get laid is really going above and beyond the call of duty."

Gloria snorted, her lips twitching in the glimmer of a smile. "You need Jesus. Get out of here."

"Yes, ma'am." Quickly logging out of her email, Laurel did as she was told. She whispered as she passed the older woman, "I'll see you in a couple of days for my lunch shift. And maybe I won't just be hoping to sleep with him by then."

"At this rate, I'll need to have my prayer mafia dedicate a whole session to you!" Gloria hollered after her.

Laurel giggled all the way down the hall. The zany characters at The Enclave were going to make this summer amazingly fun. Then again, what else had she expected at a camp full of artists?

She slung Neil's sweatshirt over her arm and jogged over to his cabin. The door was open, so she called through the screen, "Knock, knock."

"Hey!" Violet yelled back. "Come on in."

Laurel pulled open the screen door and stepped in. Hefting the hoodie in her hand, she skipped a real greeting. "I just wanted to drop this off. You forgot it in the dining room."

"Thanks." Neil set his laptop aside, hopped up from the couch, and reached for his garment. "Sorry about that. I set it on a counter when Vi almost dumped her tray and forgot to go back for it."

"That explains why none of us saw it at our table." She winked at Vi. "Especially our detail fiend."

His fingers brushed hers when he took his sweatshirt, and a sizzle buzzed over her skin. A wave of goose bumps followed in its wake, making her fight a shiver. She had a sneaking suspicion if she looked down, her nipples would be clearly visible. The fact that his gaze dropped to her breasts for just a moment told her she was right. A tiny smile played around his full lips.

"No problem," she replied, her voice a little too breathy. She cleared her throat, and turned her attention to Violet, who was hunched over a desk, her brow furrowed. "You look industrious. What are you up to?"

"I'm working on his copy edits." The teen waved a sheaf of papers in the air, covered in odd squiggles.

Laurel blinked and said slowly, "You're doing your dad's copy edits. For his novel. And you're thirteen."

"Hey, don't knock it." Neil shrugged into the hoodie and resumed his spot on the sofa. "Her grammar skills are better than mine."

Amusement trickled through Laurel. These two had the most unique father-daughter relationship. "We're ignoring child labor laws?"

"Well, we have a housekeeper at home, so cleaning and dishes and stuff are handled." He pointed out rationally, "She's got to earn her allowance somehow."

"Creative." She twisted her lips. "And kind of lazy."

"Hey, I became a parent for a reason. She needs to be well-trained so she can care for me in my old age."

The man had the driest dark humor, which surprised her because he always looked so serious and somber. He couldn't be more different than her usual type, yet she couldn't deny she was wildly attracted to him. After those kisses, she hadn't been able to get him off her mind. It had been a long time since she'd indulged in an affair, but she was hoping he might be interested. She already knew she was. Maybe it was too sudden, too fast, but her gut instinct had served her well in the past. And it told her that under his solemn exterior, Neil Graves was an explosively amazing lover. She wanted to find out if she was right about that. Their chemistry certainly lent credence to the idea.

A logical side of her brain warned that an affair could go bad before the end of a three-month program and then she'd have the awkward fun of living next door to her ex-lover. But no risk, no reward, right? She wasn't the sort of woman who was afraid of taking chances, or she'd never have gambled that a career as a painter would pay off. The odds had not been in her favor, yet here she was.

"I think I see a girl running in this direction." Neil quipped, "Who wants to bet if it's Ruth?"

Laurel pulled open the screen just as the kid came skidding through the doorway, her springy curls looking even wilder than usual.

"Hey, Violet. My grandma said I could invite you to sleepover at our cabin if you want." An appealing note entered her voice. "She baked cookies. Big ones."

"Nice." Violet tossed the copy edits aside. "These aren't due until next week. I'll be totally done before then. Okay, Dad?"

"Sure, go pack a bag. Don't forget your toothbrush," he called when she bolted for her room.

The girls were gone in under five minutes, the front door slamming shut behind them, leaving Laurel alone with Neil. For an entire night. Hot damn. She was going to kiss Gloria the next time she saw the crotchety old lady.

A bemused look formed on his face. "We decided the girls could sleepover any time. Apparently, Gloria thought there was no time like the present."

"And she sent me over here with the sweatshirt right before she sent Ruth to get Violet." Laurel tugged off the band holding her hair in a ponytail, then kicked aside her sandals. "Gloria's playing quite the matchmaker tonight."

"I'll have to thank her later." Neil rose and removed his sweatshirt, then toed off his shoes. "And I'd like to invite you for a sleepover."

"Yes, please." She untied her shorts and pushed them down over her hips. "You're done writing for the day?"

The heat in his gaze when he took in her bare legs was enough to scorch, and a throb of want went through her. It took him a long time to answer her question. "I made my projected word count at around dawn this morning. Everything else was bonus."

"Such a good boy." She pulled off her shirt and tossed it aside. All she wore was a pair of lacy panties and a matching bra. Not that she really needed a bra with her barely-A-cups, but she liked pretty lingerie as much as the next girl. From the way Neil's breath sucked in, she had a feeling he liked her pretty lingerie as well. She ran a finger along the waist of her underwear. "You know, I believe in rewarding good behavior."

"Me too," he agreed fervently. His T-shirt and cargo shorts were off so quickly she was surprised he didn't end up with fabric burn.

She stared at his thick erection, outlined starkly by his tight boxer briefs. White-hot lava flowed through her veins, and though they'd only met the day before, she felt like she'd been waiting forever for this moment to arrive. Finally. "Tell me you have condoms."

"I have a few in my toiletry case, thank God. I checked earlier." He held out his hand and, when she took it, lifted her palm to kiss and nip at her sensitive flesh.

"A few might not be enough." Tingles broke down her limbs and moisture flooded her core. Wanton need tightened some of her muscles, loosened others, readying her for sex. "I have a feeling a one-night stand isn't going to satisfy either of us. I can pick up more the next time the van goes into town."

"More is good." His lips moved up her arm to her elbow, her shoulder. "So is making very, very sure we're satisfied."

He pressed his mouth to her neck, biting down lightly. A quiver of pure desire shook her, and she tilted her head to grant him as much access as he might want. He took advantage, sliding his tongue along the length of her throat. His breath on her skin was hot, and she arched into him, pressing her curves into his harder angles. The feel of his rougher skin against her was an amazing turn-on, the crisp curls on his chest and legs rasping over her flesh.

Tipping her head back, she slipped her arms around his neck, and he took the hint, claiming her lips. The taste of him was exquisite, warm and masculine and uniquely Neil. Their tongues twined, and her heart began to race as her excitement built. Only thin layers of lace and cotton separated them, and his erection pressed insistently at her belly. She twisted, wanting to get even closer, but not wanting to break the kiss.

His palms skimmed down her back, slipping under the waistband of her panties. He palmed her backside, molded the soft globes and ran a finger between them. Then he dipped even further in, teasing flesh that was rarely open for exploration. She squeaked and squirmed, but still pushed closer and let him do whatever he wanted. As taboo as this was, it revved her up even more.

"I think we can get rid of these, don't you?" He eased her underwear down to her ankles. "Step out of them."

She did as he bid, reaching behind her to unhook her bra. "I want you naked too."

"Mmm. In a minute. You have the sweetest ass I have ever seen." He swatted one cheek, just hard enough to send tingles skipping down her skin. "Too much pain?"

She gasped, shaking her head. "No."

By stroking his fingertips over that same patch of sensitized flesh, he intensified the feeling, and she quivered. Then he moved to kneel behind her, biting and kissing the other cheek. A sound that was somewhere between a laugh and a moan escaped her. If anything, she grew wetter, needier, greedier for him. She wanted him inside her, plunging deep, making her scream with satisfaction. God, yes. That was exactly what she craved.

"Neil..."

Something about her tone must have alerted him that she was done waiting, because he rose and urged her backward onto the sofa. He stripped his boxer briefs off and settled on top of her. The weight of him pressing her down was perfect, and she wrapped her legs around his waist.

"Now. Please. Hurry." God, was that her voice begging?

"Damn it," he groaned and wrenched himself away from her, rising to his feet.

"What?" He was stopping? Now? She'd kill him.

"Condom." He stared down at her for a moment, and then bent to suck her nipple into his mouth. Her body bowed, pushing closer to him, but he pulled back. "Don't move. Stay just like that."

She sat up when he came back carrying a handful of rubbers. He dropped all but one on the coffee table and settled beside her to quickly sheath himself. She barely waited for him to be done before she straddled him. *Now, now, now.* That was all she could think, her body ruling the moment.

He held himself steady for her, and she felt the probe of his thick shaft. She braced her hands on his broad shoulders, dragging in a steadying breath as she began to sink down on him. The bulbous crest stretched her, and she rocked her hips into him. Up, down, up, down. With each pass, she took more of him. He filled her to the limit, the fit exquisite.

"Laurel." Her name on his lips was both a curse and a prayer, and a rush of power hit her.

She grinned. "Yes?"

"I...I need..." His hands bracketed her hips, his grip tight as she began to move on him.

The skin stretched taut over his sharp cheekbones, and his gray gaze was a little wild. He pulled her tighter to him on every downward plunge, as if he couldn't get close enough or deep enough. The rough hair at his groin stimulated her sex as she ground herself against him. God, it felt good. Amazing. She wanted to hold out, to make it last longer, but didn't think she could. Her body demanded gratification, and all she could do was ride out the carnal storm.

Sweat slipped down their skin, their gasps and groans echoing in the cabin. She dug her nails into his shoulders, pushing herself to greater speeds. She was so close, so very close to that wicked edge. "Please...please..."

"Come for me." He smacked her ass again, sending a shockwave of pleasure-pain through her. Her head fell back and she sobbed out her ecstasy, her inner muscles fisting in rhythmic pulses around his thick length.

The sound he made was like a human volcano erupting, as if all restraints had ripped free. With startling speed, he tumbled her onto the couch, shoved deeper inside her than he'd been before, and began to ride her hard. This was no slow taking, but a swift, raw possession.

And she loved it.

Passion rebuilt, higher and higher. She cinched her legs tight around his hips, lifting into his thrusts. Their skin slapped together, the sound loud and obscene and erotic.

A muscle ticked in his cheek. "I can't wait."

He reached between them and thumbed her nub, which was more than enough to send her into orbit again. Her body bowed, a cry breaking from her throat. Her sex milked the length of his shaft. He continued moving, racing for his own completion. Each plunge sent aftershocks quaking through her body, dragging her orgasm out forever, so that one blended into the next and she was consumed by the uncontrollable pleasure.

His thrusts grew rougher, and then a shudder rippled through him. He drove deep one last time and froze. A long, low moan escaped him as he sank down on top of her. She held him close, both of them gasping. Her heart thudding against her ribs, and sweat glued their bodies together.

After a minute, he shifted so they were on their sides facing each other, and she could breathe easier, but he was still plastered against her from chest to thigh and their legs tangled. The rush of endorphins had left her a little giddy, and she couldn't have wiped the grin off her face if she tried. Her body felt soft and languid and just a little bruised from where his hands had gripped her.

Totally worth it.

Sucking in air, she said, "Just so you know?"

"Yeah?" His voice with still a little hoarse, his breath rushing in and out.

She tapped the cleft in his chin. "You have excellent throw down, Graves. Even without the etchings."

And that was the first time she got to see him double up with laughter, almost falling off the sofa. There was really nothing like making a quiet man laugh his ass off. It felt almost as good as the sex.

Which was really saying something.

CHAPTER FIVE

"**W**hich cabin are we looking for?" Violet asked as she and Ruth trailed behind Neil.

"6C," he answered. It was Sunday morning, and he'd been told his mentee had arrived the night before, but he hadn't run into her yet. Time to be proactive, since the program officially kicked off tomorrow. All participants were supposed to have shown up by now, and there was an official meet-and-mingle party for everyone tonight. Laurel was going as his date, and Violet had decided she'd rather hang out with Ruth than a bunch of adults. Gloria wanted nothing to do with a party, so she'd volunteered to have Violet over for the night.

Of course, Neil and Vi had hosted Ruth the night before. Two girls under his tiny cabin roof had put the kibosh on any writing and any sexy times with Laurel, but the painter had come over anyway, shown off her skills with the brush by doing some fancy stuff with nail polish, and Neil had been in charge of securing popcorn from the lodge. Luckily, there was a vending machine with bags of Orville Redenbacher's and a microwave in the dining room, because there was no way in hell he was pissing off Gloria by raiding her kitchen. He valued his skin too much. The woman had a real fondness for knives, after all.

His daughter caught up with him. "How do you even know your apprentice is home, Dad?"

He slung an arm around her shoulder. "There's only one way to find out."

"I bet she's home." Ruth kicked a rock, and it skipped down the dirt path. "She wasn't in the lodge."

The roads around The Enclave were arranged like four spokes on a wheel, with the lodge as the hub. One road led to town, and the other three were lined with cabins. All the As were on one road, Bs on another, Cs on the last. Grassy meadows and mature trees filled the gaps in between. The scent of pine hung in the warm air, so different from LA's perpetual layer of smog.

When Neil and his daughter had passed the main lodge on the way to the C row, Ruth had come jogging out to join them. She really did go everywhere at a run, but Vi appeared to have a devoted new friend, which pleased him. Violet had had to leave all her friends behind in Maine when she'd moved in with him, and she hadn't yet made any close connections with the kids in southern California. It was excellent to see her bonding with someone in her age group.

"I hope this mentee woman is chill," Vi commented. "Or your summer will suck."

"I'm sure I'll get along with her." They approached the correct cabin, and he was about to knock when the sound of voices made him walk over to look around the far side of the building. A woman sat in a folding chair with two toddlers playing in the grass at her feet.

"Mateo, give your sister back her Legos. Those aren't yours." She heaved an exasperated sigh. "Jina, honey, don't put that in your mouth. We don't eat rocks."

The teeny girl shoved the rocks to one side of her mouth, making her look like a lopsided chipmunk. "Why?"

Without missing a beat, the mother replied, "They're bad for your teeth."

Neil didn't quite manage to suppress his amused snort at that answer. He remembered when Violet's response to anything was *why*. Actually, he wasn't sure his daughter had ever grown out of that phase. She questioned everything. Not a bad trait for an adult, but it made him want to strangle the teen now and then.

Little Jina spat out a black, chunky blob of muddy pebbles.

The woman looked up when he snorted. She brought a hand up to shield her eyes from the bright sunlight, squinting to see him. The sun was behind him, so he doubted she got a clear look at him, but he stepped out from behind the cabin.

Violet and Ruth seemed to have vanished for the moment. A quick backward glance showed them following a fleeing lizard.

"Hello. Sorry to intrude. I was just flashing back to my daughter's toddler years." He moved forward to shake the woman's hand. Unless he missed his guess, this was his new apprentice.

She gave his fingers a quick squeeze, then used her T-shirt to wipe the dirt from her daughter's chin. "My twin terrors have just hit the terrible twos. I'm not sure the hubby and I will survive them turning three."

He laughed. "It is a truly special time in child development."

"Special," she agreed, making air quotes.

"Exactly."

"I'm Helen Cho. And you're Neil Graves. Let's try this again." She stood, brushed off her cropped pants, and offered him a firm handshake. "I'll be your mentee for the summer."

"So it seems." He grinned. "I liked the sample pages The Enclave sent to me."

"Oh…oh." She fanned her face. "You're gonna make me blush. Or cry."

"There's no crying in this mentoring relationship. That's my only real rule." It wasn't as if they could hug it out like he did with Violet, so he was really hoping for no tears. Time for a subject switch. "I understand your husband is here for the program as well. What does he do?"

"I see what you did there." Helen wagged a finger at him. "My husband is Pedro Diaz—"

That name rang a bell. "The sculptor?"

"That's the one." Pride suffused her voice. "He's doing some amazing things modernizing the low-reliefs that were part of some ancient Mesoamerican cultures."

Neil had no idea what that might mean, but the director of *Dead and Gone* had owned several of Diaz's pieces. "I like his work."

"Me too. He's the laidback, serene one in the family." She grinned. "Whereas I want to bring some of the Korean horror film motifs into my first novel. Which is why I jumped at the chance to have the king of thrillers mentor me."

"I hope I live up to the hype." Neil rubbed the back of his neck.

"You will." She waited a beat. "Or I'll sic the Cho-Diaz twins on you."

He arched an eyebrow. "A terrifying prospect, I'm sure."

"I have eyes in the back of my head, Mateo." She twisted at the waist to give her son A Look. "Stop that."

The kid froze, his hand outstretched toward his sister's Legos. He yanked away and studiously focused on zooming his toy truck across the grass.

Violet and her partner in crime popped up at his elbow. His daughter held up her hand. "Check out the cool rock we found, Dad. I'm taking it back to LA as a souvenir."

"Whatever makes you happy, honey." He shrugged. Of all the things she could want as a souvenir, that was probably the least expensive.

Vi looked his mentee over. "So, you're my dad's victim for this trip?"

"I'm creepily excited by that prospect." Helen rocked back on her heels, her expression gleeful.

Nodding sagely, the teen replied, "Well, horror writers are creepy."

Neil raised his eyes heavenward while Helen chortled.

Looking from the woman to her children, Violet offered, "Let me know if you ever need babysitting. I come cheap."

"My twins might kill you—you'd be outnumbered."

"I can help," Ruth said. "That evens things up."

"Sure." Vi patted her friend's shoulder. "We'll split the cash."

Helen's gaze met his and her brow rose in question. He shrugged. "I'm okay with it, but you'll need to check with Ruth's grandmother before you split anything."

"I'll ask her," Ruth promised. "But she'll say yes. I babysit my neighbor's kids at home all the time. She can't take them with her when she goes to yoga."

"You guys can practice now while Helen and I chat." Neil waved them toward the toddlers. "We need to sort out how we want to get this mentorship started."

He already had a hunch he was going to like Helen. She was clearly a bit warped, which made her one of his favorite kinds of people. The more he listened to what she wanted to write, the more he was sure this was going to be a good experience. He wished for the millionth time that he didn't have one book in edits, another not finished but overdue to his publisher, and the script due at the end of the program. One less thing on his plate might make this mentorship a lot more fun, but he had a feeling between grumpy Gloria, running Ruth, horror Helen, and lovely Laurel, he and Vi were going to have a summer they'd never forget.

Okay, that was way too much alliteration, even for a writer. He wasn't a poet, for God's sake.

"I've never shopped in a general store before. Is it like a Walmart?" Violet positioned herself between Laurel and Neil as they headed toward the lodge. They were supposed to be meeting Mimi to drive into town for some shopping.

"I'm not sure," Neil answered. "If they have a little bit of everything, maybe it's a like a mini Wally World?"

"Maybe. We'll find out soon, huh?" Vi turned to walk backward in front of Laurel. "Guess what? We met Dad's mentee right after breakfast. She's nice. Ruth and I are going to babysit her twins for her. They're two years old. Kinda evil and really cute."

"Sounds about right for that age. My nephew will turn two in August." A little pang hit her. How could he be almost two already? It was just yesterday he'd been born. Pulling herself back to the present, she glanced around. "Where is Ruth, by the way? I pretty much assumed she'd be coming with us. I thought you two had been surgically attached at the hip."

"Hardly." Vi rolled her eyes. "She left for church with her grandma a few minutes ago."

"Ah. My family isn't very religious." They worshipped status more than anything else. Laurel could count on one hand the number of times she'd been to church with a friend's family. It just wasn't part of her life experience, but maybe she should tag along one Sunday to meet Gloria's prayer mafia. Because...prayer mafia.

"We're not religious either." Violet flapped a hand to indicate Neil and herself. "I think Mom's parents were, but I never met them."

"You did, you just don't remember." Neil slid his hands into the back pockets on his cargo shorts. "Their boat capsized when you were...maybe eighteen months old or so."

"Mom didn't talk about them much. Like, at all." She faced forward and matched her father's stride.

Something dark flashed through his gaze, and his jaw flexed before he spoke. "She didn't have the greatest relationship with them. They only visited twice right after you were born, and we never saw them again."

"Wow." Vi looked surprised and disheartened. "That sucks."

Laurel couldn't agree with her more. Even her own mother managed to be a better grandparent. Hell, her dad had seen Nicky more often than that.

"What about your parents?" Laurel queried. Maybe they were better at parenting and grandparenting.

"They were awesome." A sad smile curved his lips. "Cancer got them both, unfortunately. Dad died about ten years ago—testicular cancer. Mom passed four years ago. Lung cancer. She smoked like a chimney from the time she was fifteen until the day she died. Tried to quit a million times, but it just never stuck."

"Dad donates tons of money to cancer charities and cancer research." Violet pressed herself to his side, and he gave her a one-armed hug.

"That's a great way to honor them." Laurel wanted to hug him too, but she'd refrained from public displays of affection in the days they'd been sleeping together. Maybe that was something they needed to talk about. Were they just secret lovers or were they having some kind of summer romance? The difference was mostly in how they acted in front of others. She hadn't thought the distinction was important, but in the tiny community of this artist retreat, it made a huge difference.

The big blue van owned by The Enclave was parked in its usual space beside the lodge. They were cutting across the grass toward the vehicle when Mimi stepped out of the building to meet them.

"Laurel. Do you have a moment?" The perpetually perky woman looked distressed, wringing her hands.

A twinge of anxiety hit Laurel. Something was wrong, but what? A hundred possibilities ran through her mind, each worse than the next. Her brother was injured, her nephew had had an accident. She flicked a glance at Neil and Violet. "Why don't you go ahead? I'll catch up."

"The van is unlocked." Mimi's smile was a mere shadow of its normal self. "We'll join you in a sec."

"KK, I get the front seat." Violet dodged around her dad. He followed more slowly, concern in his gaze when his eyes met Laurel's. She appreciated the sentiment, but the longer he lingered the longer her wait was until Mimi spit out whatever she was holding back.

"What's up?" Laurel pulled the end of her ponytail over her shoulder, fiddling with it nervously.

"The artist you're paired with is delayed." More hand wringing, and Mimi started to pace in a tight circle. "A volcano erupted near where he's vacationing in Asia and they have to wait for the sky to clear before they can fly out, but with all the other people trying to get out too, who knows when he'll be here? It could be a couple of days or a week—we just don't know."

"The important part is he's safe and unharmed, right?" Laurel soothed, more than a little thrilled that it was nothing more serious than this. "As long as he still intends to participate in the program, then I don't mind a delay. I'll just work on some of my own pieces in the meantime."

Relief flooded Mimi's expression. "You're not upset?"

"Being a successful artist doesn't make me an entitled drama queen."

She sighed, her shoulders relaxing. "Even the not-yet-successful ones have flipped out on me for less."

"Well, I can be a bigger jerk next time if it makes you feel more comfortable." Laurel couldn't help making the offer, just to watch the horror cross the other woman's face. Yes, she was a little evil—she could admit it.

"No, no. That's all right." Mimi held out her hands as it to fend off the very idea. "I usually love my job except when I have to deliver bad news."

"Was anyone hurt in the eruption? Because that would be the real bad news." Perspective was a good thing. Art really didn't mean much if you were too dead to care.

"Not that anyone's reported. It was a pretty remote mountain. It's just messing up local air travel."

"Okay, then. I'm sure it'll all be fine. Don't stress." Laurel reached over and squeezed Mimi's wrist. "Let me know if you get any other updates on my apprentice. Now, let's go shopping."

"Excellent!" Mimi bounced toward the van, chipperness restored.

Well, it looked like she had some free time for at least a couple of days. Maybe she could check out that lake Ruth had mentioned. Laurel had brought her swimsuit—a bikini she thought Neil might really enjoy. It made her butt look amazing, and she'd noticed he had a real fondness for that portion of her anatomy.

With that thought, she turned to join the others. It was time to get this show on the road.

Ten minutes later, Laurel grinned and pressed her nose to the window of the van. "I'd never have guessed I'd be so giddy to go to a one-gas-station town."

"Gas station slash deli slash general store, don't forget," Mimi called from the driver's seat.

"The groundskeeper told me they have fishing supplies and live bait too." Violet twisted around in the passenger seat to make a disgusted face at her dad and Laurel. "If I have to kill my food's food, I think I'll be a vegetarian."

"That's the cycle of life, honey."

"We learned all about cycles in school. Girl cycles." Her expression went from disgusted to nauseated. "Everybody makes all these cycles sound all natural but, like, they're no fun for anyone. Blood, death, gross."

Laurel sucked in her cheeks to keep from laughing. "Eloquent, sweetie. You've got a real way with words. No wonder you want to be a writer."

"I totally do." The teen preened a bit, then turned back around.

The three of them had spent every meal together since they'd arrived. And a lot of time in between. Laurel had to remind herself that they weren't some sort of instant family, even though that was what it felt like. The thought made warmth expand in her chest, which was one hundred percent stupid. They'd go their separate ways when the program was over, period, end of story.

"Blood, death, gross," Neil whispered in her ear. "They're gonna put that on my tombstone."

She bumped her knee against his. "*Girl cycles* is always an option instead."

"Pass." He had his arm across the back of the bench seat they shared, and he stroked his long fingers along the top of her shoulder and collarbone.

She swallowed, heat beginning to pool in her belly. One reason they'd both been eager to come along on Mimi's trip to town was that they were out of condoms. They'd run out on Saturday, after a nooner while Ruth and Violet were swimming. Which meant everything since then had been pure erotic torment and a whole lot of frustration. She'd also found out exactly how talented Neil was with his hands and mouth. Even then, she wanted the real thing. Neil, inside her, thrusting until they were sweaty and groaning and hurtling toward orgasm. She shuddered, squeezing her thighs together as wicked heat began to build.

Setting her hand on his thigh, she dug her nails in. A warning to stop teasing her. She was going to explode if she didn't get some relief soon. He shifted his leg, which didn't help. They were both wearing shorts, and having the rough hair on his leg rasp over her skin just made her shiver, reminding her of more intimate moments when she'd experienced the same sensation.

His fingertips continued to move in slow circles over her neck, along the curve of her ear, down her nape. Waves of tingles skipped over her skin, and her breathing sped. God, she wanted him. And she wanted to kick him because he knew exactly what he was doing to her.

Her toes curled in her sneakers, and she hissed, "You'll get it for this later, Graves."

"Looking forward to it, Patton," he murmured and tugged on her earlobe. "Get me good, promise?"

After dipping her hand below the hem of his shorts, she yanked on a few of his leg hairs. He yelped loudly, but Laurel was all wide-eyed innocence when Mimi and Violet looked back.

"What's wrong, Dad?"

"The seatbelt pinched me." He tugged at the bottom of his shorts and shot Laurel a dirty look. She returned a guileless smile.

Violet's glance was sympathetic. "Ouch."

"We're here," Mimi sang out with her unflagging cheer. She pulled the van off the highway, and they bumped over a few potholes to reach the single gas pump. "You guys go ahead. I'll fill up, then do some Enclave shopping. Meet back at the van in forty-five minutes."

"This is a town?" Vi squinted dubiously.

Not that anyone could blame her for being unconvinced. There was the giant warehouse of a general store, and three clapboard buildings strung alongside the highway. That was it.

"There's a post office across the street," Mimi pointed out. "That officially makes it a town, I think."

"Well, I want to see the glory of the general store. It's got to be awesome. Look at it." The sides of the building featured faded murals of fly fishermen, deer about to be bagged by hunters, old miners with pickaxes, a view of the mountains, a giant American flag, and a totally incongruous pair of flamingos. Someone had a sense of humor. Or a break from sanity. Either one could be interesting, if it was the right kind of crazy.

Neil crawled out in front of her, and it was difficult to resist pinching his ass, but she managed. After slinging her purse over her shoulder, she took his hand and let him help her out. Not that she needed the assistance, but she liked touching him. Well, she liked touching him knowing she was going to have the most enormous box of condoms in her possession soon. Or she'd clean out the store of all their little boxes. She didn't care how, but a lot of rubbers were coming back to her cabin. And she intended to use all of them with Neil in very, very creative ways.

Violet dragged Neil off as soon as they entered the store, and Laurel grabbed a basket and made a beeline for the area labeled Pharmacy/Personal Health. The condom selection was surprisingly large, but then again…what else were people going to do except each other when it snowed in for the winter? She picked the most entertaining box she could, shoved it in the basket over her arm, and then raced to snag a few other items and beat everyone to the checkout.

After paying, she shoved all her purchases into the canvas bag she'd brought along. A quick trip out to the unlocked van and she'd hidden everything safely under the seat. Not that she was ashamed of sleeping with Neil, but she didn't want to face knowing looks from Mimi, or worse, questions from his teen daughter. If anyone was having the awkward sex talk with Violet, it was Neil. If she wanted to talk teenage crushes, Laurel was game, but discussions about Laurel banging Violet's dad. Yeah, no. Not going there.

She ran smack into the man in question as she slipped back into the general store.

"Already done? You have over thirty minutes left." He grinned. "What did you get?"

"You should finish your shopping and quit interrogating me." Flipping her ponytail over her shoulder, she gave him a haughty look. "Where's your daughter?"

"She's busy. I asked her to help Mimi do the shopping for The Enclave. Back to our original topic." Leaning closer, his dark hair fell forward to cover his face and his voice dropped to the dark, sinful tone he used in bed. "What did you get, sweetheart?"

"A flavored variety pack." She fluttered her eyelashes. "I like to keep things interesting. There's strawberry, watermelon…even bubble gum. Think it's encouraging me to blow something?"

A ruddy flush darkened his face, and dangerous need flashed wildly in his gaze. "I know which flavor I want you to start with."

"I might make you beg first. I think you'd look good on your knees, Graves."

"Christ," he sighed, closing his eyes. "You're trying to kill me."

"Maybe." She tugged at a shoulder strap on the backpack he wore. "Is that a problem?"

"Yes, a huge problem." He took her arm and began propelling her across the store.

She went without protest. "Where exactly are we going?"

"Here." He led her under a staircase in the back and thrust her through a doorway. He followed her in, flipped a light switch, and shut and locked the door behind them.

Blinking in the sudden change of light, she took in her surroundings. "You need to pee?"

"Nope." He tugged her over to the sink. "Put your hands on the counter."

Her lips parted. "You're seriously thinking we should—"

"Twenty-seven minutes left." He shrugged out of his pack and hung it from a hook on the wall. His gaze met hers in the mirror, an impish challenge shining there. "Yes or no, Patton?"

Damn, she'd never been able to walk away from a dare. It had landed her in hot water more than once as a child, but how much trouble could she really get into now? Embarrassment was the worst possibility. Totally worth the risk.

She set her purse on the counter and flipped open the button on her cotton shorts. Then she froze. "My condoms are already in the van."

"Luckily, I got some too." He rifled through his bag and came up with a long strip of perforated foil packets. He pulled one free. "Not flavored, but they should get the job done."

"Hurry." Because they didn't have much time and she'd missed this since they'd run out of protection. She wanted him inside her. The sense of the forbidden was titillating, exciting, and her sex clenched, going slick in seconds.

Yep, she was definitely going to do this. Even though it was utterly insane.

Sanity was overrated.

T his was one of the stupidest things he'd done in a very long time, and yet he had no desire to stop.

He tossed the condom on the counter, then fitted himself against Laurel's back. The sweet curve of her backside nestled against his rising erection, and the feeling was about ten shades of perfect. He swept one hand up her side, sliding over to bracket her jaw, and tilted her head toward him. He needed to taste her, and he melded his mouth with hers, slipping his tongue between her lips. Her fingers closed around his wrist, but he wrapped his other arm around her waist, holding her tight. He nipped and sucked at her lips, feasting on her mouth while he felt her excitement increase. She whimpered softly, her body beginning to writhe against his. The feel of her backside rubbing over his erection made him groan.

His heart rate increased, blood rushing like a hot river through his veins. Desperate need was a living thing inside him, and he had to touch her, claim her. After dipping his fingers under the hem of her T-shirt, he let his hand glide up the soft, soft skin of her stomach and could only groan when he found she wasn't wearing a bra. He cupped her breast and the tight crest stabbed into his palm. He fondled her, rotating his grip to stimulate her nipple.

He released her chin and moved that hand down to her shorts. The top was already unfastened, so it was simple enough to nudge the zipper down and ease his fingers into her panties. Then he pressed through the soft thatch of hair to her wet folds.

When he pinched her nub, she ripped her mouth from his. "Now. Right now. No more teasing, or I might have to kill you."

"We can't have that." He plucked the condom up from the counter and wrestled his clothes out of the way to roll it on. The way she stared at his erection didn't help him steady his hands at all.

Once he was covered, he grabbed her hips and spun her to face the sink again. Then he hooked his fingers into the back of her shorts and yanked them and her panties down around her thighs.

"*Now*," she demanded again, bending a little to brace her hands on the counter.

"Yes." He grasped his erection and positioned himself, then pressed forward one slow inch at a time. The hot, slick clasp of her sex around his shaft was so amazing, he thought he might die. "Ah, Jesus, Laurel. That feels…"

"So damn good." Her gaze met his in the mirror, those dark eyes still holding all the mysteries in the world. She grinned, sweet and sexy and all kinds of naughty.

He winked back. God, he liked her so much. She was a rare breath of fresh air in his sometimes stifled, overloaded life. But that thought was far too deep for a moment like this.

He withdrew as slowly as he'd entered her, only to plunge back in. His body urged him to go faster, harder and he gave in to his needs. Their skin slapped together, a harsh crack of sound in the tiled room. His lungs worked like bellows, trying to suck in enough air as he plunged into her. An arrested expression crossed her face, and her eyes slid closed, as if she were savoring every moment of the experience. The smothered little noises that broke from her throat told him how close she was getting. He was teetering on the edge himself, but he needed her right there with him.

"Laurel," he whispered, and she opened her eyes, their gazes clashing in the mirror. "I want to see you come."

"You won't have to wait long." She bit her lip to suppress a moan, and her face flushed a deep red. Her gaze sharpened and then lost focus, a shiver took her, and he felt the hot clench and release of her channel around his shaft. The sheer ecstasy that swept over her expression was one of the loveliest things he'd ever seen, and one of the most erotic.

He drove into her again and again, wanting to drag her climax out, wanting to keep that look on her face. But pleasuring her meant pleasuring himself, and his control was crumbling fast. One, two, three more thrusts and he broke, coming hard, and fighting to hold back a groan.

Christ, this was amazing. His head dropped forward to rest between her shoulder blades, and he had to struggle to get his breathing under control. Several minutes passed before his heart stopped racing and his limbs stopped shaking. He couldn't remember the last time a woman had nearly brought him to his knees, the orgasm had been so intense. He knew he wanted more of this, of her. Maybe more than he should, but that bridge had been burned and there was no going back. If he was honest, he'd admit he didn't want to go back...sex with Laurel was one of the most heart-racing, thrilling things he'd ever done.

Pushing himself upright, he asked, "Are you okay?"

"Very." She tugged the band from her hair. Somehow it had slipped partially free of its restraints. "I liked the way you looked when you lost it."

"Likewise." His dropped a kiss on her shoulder. "We should clean up."

He stepped away to do just that, and when he glanced up again

Laurel was trying to refasten her ponytail. The results were...reasonably good, though she still appeared a bit mussed and flushed. A glance in the mirror showed he also looked far too mellow for a man who'd just been shopping. He finger-combed his hair, tucked in his shirt and zipped his shorts, and that would have to do.

She picked up her purse. "Ready?"

He slung his backpack over his shoulder and moved to peek out the door. "Coast is clear. Let's make a run for it."

Amusement lilted in her voice. "Should we stagger our exits so people don't know we were in here together? We can synchronize our watches."

"Let's not get too complicated." He grabbed her hand and pulled her along with him.

They made it out of the store without some irate shopkeeper chasing them, so he figured they'd made a clean getaway. Nice. It was always fun to indulge in prurient behavior with zero consequences.

Violet stuck her head out of the window when they approached the van. "Dad, I found another cool rock behind the store. It's got, like, red stripes in it." But then her eyes narrowed in suspicion. "Hey, where did you guys go? You were gone for a while."

Laurel checked her watch. "We're right on time, Vi. Don't let your need to be early freak you out."

It wasn't an answer to her question, but Mimi rushed up just then and interrupted. "All right, campers. The stock boy loaded everything in the van for me, and Gloria wants some of these supplies pronto. Let's get back on the road. Did you guys get everything you needed?"

"Definitely." Neil gave her a mild smile, and Laurel elbowed him subtly as she climbed into the van before him.

Mimi turned on the radio and got Vi and Laurel to sing bad country music with her. Off-key. Neil tried not to wince, but the noise was good cover. He leaned over to Laurel and commented quietly, "It's going to be hard to hide what we're up to. At best, it'll soon be an open secret."

"I was thinking the same thing earlier." She let her head fall back against the seat, then rolled it to face him. "Are you concerned about Violet knowing?"

"She's known when I was with other women before. I don't hide things from her. You'd be the first of my lovers who had a relationship with her, so that would be new." He tapped his fingertips on his thigh. "I don't have a problem with her knowing we're…dating…if you don't."

"Are we calling this dating?" Her wide eyes gave nothing away, so he had no way of guessing what she thought.

"Not that I get to take you out to dinner or bring you flowers while we're here, but I'd say yes. We're dating." He swallowed hard, suddenly nervous and sure he was going to get dumped by someone who wasn't yet his girlfriend. "That's my opinion. You might have a different take on things."

She ran her fingers down his forearm, the caress lighter than a whisper. "I'm okay with the dating label. For the summer. I can't commit to anything beyond that."

"And you're all right with people knowing we're using the dating label?" he prompted. "Just for the summer."

While he hadn't expected to deal with a romantic relationship during this program, now that he was confronted with the possibility, he wanted the details nailed down. Not his usual MO, but nothing about his reaction to Laurel had been usual so far.

"Yes, people can know. Including Violet." Her gaze went dead serious. "But you need to actually talk to her about it, find out if she's really okay with it."

It had never occurred to him not to talk to Vi. This wasn't something he wanted his kid hearing about through the grapevine. As he'd said, it would be an open secret if they didn't go public. Vi deserved to hear about it from him. "And if she's not okay with this?"

Laurel shrugged. "We keep this to the very occasional booty call, and try very hard not to get caught, so we don't become fodder for the gossip mill. Which would mean no more of what we just did. It'd be too big a risk."

"Fair enough. I'll speak to her." His respect for her notched up a little more, liking that she understood his daughter's feelings would have to take precedence over a short-term relationship that hadn't even fully formed yet. Luckily, he was about ninety-eight percent certain Vi would be ecstatic to have Laurel around even more often.

"Hey, you stopped singing!" Mimi glanced in the rearview mirror.

Laurel waved back. "I didn't like that song."

She rejoined the choir of caterwauling, and he tried not to whimper all the way back to the lodge.

Thank God she was a better painter than singer.

CHAPTER SIX

T hey were starting to become experts in the quickie.

It had been two weeks, and any time Vi was busy with something else, Laurel found herself in Neil's arms. His daughter had definitely been okay with them dating, but Laurel wasn't quite ready to stay the night with Vi there. So, they specialized in afternoon delights. And it was delightful. It was hot and amazing and got better every time. How was that even possible? Shouldn't the passion be fizzling? It usually did. Annoying little habits usually became more noticeable, fights over nothing tended to crop up, and they no longer ended in make-up sex.

But none of that happened with Neil.

The only thing that scared her was his workaholic tendencies. It reminded her far too much of her father, and anything that smacked of Robert Patton made her more than a little leery. She'd always made damn sure she never, never dated a man like Dad.

Except...she had the horrible suspicion that outside of the disconnected oasis that was The Enclave, Neil was the same kind of man. Always too busy, always on call, never really relaxing, never really giving all his attention to a woman, even when she was right in front of him.

The last thing Laurel needed was a man who put her last on his priority list. That path had almost led her brother to divorce, and had led to her parents' detached, chilly partnership. She should know better than to even consider wanting more than hot sex from a guy like Neil.

But she wanted. She couldn't help it, and that scared her to death.

"Ugh." She let her head fall back and closed her eyes. She'd been staring at her unfinished painting for several minutes, lost in thought instead of her creative process.

The problem was, she'd become more emotionally involved than she'd expected to. Neil was busy all the time, so she'd figured it would be no more than an indulgence now and then. But it wasn't. There were meals together, there were kitchen shifts with Neil, there was helping Violet with her book, trying to make sure Neil had quiet time to get his writing done, but also getting him to unwind a little too. She felt like she was part of something important when she was with them—a valued, needed member of a family. Something she'd never felt with her own family. Well...Tate had always done his best, but her parents? Yeah, she was unessential.

Stop it, Laurel. She blew out a breath. She needed to work. The hours were ticking down until she had a meeting with her apprentice. The man was an odd little duck, but his work had promise. She wasn't exactly going to have the friendly relationship Neil had with Helen, though. Laurel could barely get her mentee to speak or even look up from his canvas, and thus far, she'd never seen him leave his cabin. She met with him there, period. It was weird.

Sitting back on her stool, she surveyed her work so far. Not bad. Her style was identifiable not by her subject matter, but by her unique use of color and her refusal to paint anything exactly as it appeared in reality. Everything was just a little exaggerated, a little larger than life. Right now, she was toying with macro-painting, her riff on macrophotography. She wasn't sure how long she'd stick with this phase, but it was fun while it lasted.

In this piece, a single tree dominated the mountains around it, eclipsing the entire forest. She dipped her brush into green paint and added details to the leaves. Pushing everything else from her mind, she forced herself to settle and focus on the task at hand. She had years of discipline to draw on—there was always something else competing for attention, always something or someone that seemed more pressing than a single day of painting. But those days added up, and she had had to learn to set boundaries with herself and others.

This was her priority right now. No one was maimed or dying, and the world wouldn't end if she ignored it for a while.

So she lost herself in the movement of her arm, the flicks of her wrist, the layers and texture she added to her canvas. All those other problems—real or imagined—would have to wait.

She didn't know how much later it was when her screen door creaked open. It wasn't yet time to meet with her apprentice, because she'd set an alarm on her phone—the only real use for the thing out here in the reception-free boondocks.

"Oh, she's painting," Violet whispered, and the door *thunked* as she backed out and let it close. "We should leave her alone."

A soft rumble came from Neil, though he pitched his voice low enough that Laurel couldn't make out the words.

She grinned, dropped her brush in a can of turpentine, and swung around. "Did you guys need something?"

"Nope." Vi came in again, shrugged out of a backpack and dropped it against the nearest wall. "We just wanted to say hi."

"Hi, there. How's your day going?" Checking her cell phone, Laurel decided it was a good time to clean up her brushes and workspace. Her meeting was about an hour away.

"Not bad." Violet tipped her head and eyed Laurel's canvas. "Dad's been super busy though. I'm pretty sure a whole herd of elephants could show up and he wouldn't notice unless they, like, stepped on his laptop and stole his pad of paper."

As if to illustrate the teen's point, Neil had already sunk down on Laurel's small loveseat and was scribbling away in his notebook. Yep, he was definitely in the zone.

"I can hear you," he said, but didn't look up, just kept writing.

Laurel slid a glance at Vi. "How did you even get him out of the house?"

"I'm not sure he even knows he's out of the house."

"Still not deaf, ladies, but thanks for the vote of confidence." Again, no break in work, and no eye contact.

Something about that didn't sit well with Laurel. Too many years of her own father ignoring his children in favor of some important court case or other. She pushed the unpleasant memories away and finished cleaning the oil paint from her brushes.

Violet hoisted herself onto Laurel's stool but faced away from the canvas. "Hey, Dad, since you're listening and all... Can we go into Denver? Pretty please?"

"Why?" He frowned at his paper, jotting down a few more words.

"It's Ruth birthday soon." Vi swung her legs, thumping her heels against the stool's bottom rung. "I want to get her something she mentioned she wanted, but it's at a little store that doesn't sell its stuff online, so I need to go there to buy it."

"Denver's a pretty long drive, and we don't have a car." He sighed, sat back on the sofa, and met his daughter's gaze. "You can't find anything she'd like at the general store or online and have it delivered?"

Violet looked crestfallen, and Laurel's heart clenched so tight she could barely breathe. Christ, how many times had that same expression crossed her face when her father picked work over her? How many times had she been overlooked by everyone in her family except her brother? She just...couldn't let Violet feel that way, like no one cared, like she didn't matter.

The teen tucked a lock of hair behind her ear. "But...I really, really, really wanted to get this gift. It's the perfect one. Why would I look for something less perfect?"

Neil sighed again, the sound resigned, and opened his mouth to speak, but Laurel jumped in first.

"I'll go with you." She added hastily, "I'm sure we can work something out with Mimi about the car thing."

Neil's brows snapped together, and he stated emphatically, "I was about to say I'll go."

He would? She blinked. And there was that awkward moment where her past came roaring in to pee all over her present. The way he stared at her told her she was in trouble. *Well, damn.*

"We can all go," Violet enthused, quickly over her dejection and oblivious to the undercurrent of tension running between the two adults. "It'll be awesome. Saturday?"

"Let me talk to Mimi," Neil replied. "Why don't you grab your Kindle and go read outside under the tree? You said you wanted to finish the how-to book about writing mysteries."

"Mmm. I'm feeling more fiction today." She hopped off the stool, dug around in her backpack, and came out with her e-reader. "I could totally do an old Nancy Drew. Those stories are awesome-awful."

"Have fun." Neil swept a hand toward the miniscule closet. "Maybe see if Laurel's okay with you borrowing an extra blanket or towel to lay on?"

"Sure, that's fine." Laurel tried to smile but failed.

"KK." The teen grabbed a folded square of terrycloth from the closet and pushed out the screen door.

The moment she was gone, Neil turned to Laurel. "So, what was that about?"

Double damn. She winced. "I'm sorry. I shouldn't have assumed."

"It's fine—I'm not mad, just confused." He dropped his notebook on the loveseat and rose to his feet. "It was obvious this was important to Vi—for whatever teenage reason I may never understand, but important, nonetheless. Why would you think I don't care about my daughter's feelings? What gave you that impression?"

"Nothing you did," she rushed to assure him. "It's personal baggage I'm carrying around from my childhood."

That incisive gaze speared her, and she suddenly wished that he was the light and fluffy kind of guy she normally dated. The ones who were a little too self-involved to dig into her motivations, who were only too happy to attribute everything to artistic angst. Not Neil. Nope, he was going to ask questions.

"You've mentioned your dad is a jerk. He ignored you, even when things were important to you?"

"More or less." She focused on arranging her brushes, cursing herself for jumping to conclusions when she knew Neil was a great father—one of the many reasons she adored him—and putting herself in a situation where she had to justify her actions.

"And your mom?" Neil prodded. "Bad parental relations all around?"

She let out a long, weary breath and met his gaze. "My relationship with my parents is...complicated. We love each other—or they love me as much as they're capable of loving anyone—but we really don't like each other.”

“Ouch.” Sympathy shone in his gray eyes.

“Yeah. They hate that I’m an artist and not a high-priced lawyer like my dad. Or at least a lawyer’s wife, like my mom. They want me in the country club set. I couldn’t think of a life I’d want less.”

A dark eyebrow quirked upward. “Homeless bum?”

“Okay, yes.” She rolled her eyes. “I’d want that less. Though I’m fairly sure the parental units thought that’s what I was aiming for when I decided to be a painter.”

“It’s not easy making a living in the arts.” He strolled up to look at her half-finished painting, then glanced at her. “I admit I’d feel better if Vi wanted to be a lawyer. I can understand your parents’ concern.”

The smile she gave him was tight, her tone defensive. “You’d get along with them well, then.”

She tugged off the paint-splattered smock that protected her tank top, set her brushes aside, and avoided his gaze.

“I’m not saying they’re right, or that they shouldn’t have supported your choices. Or that they should still nag you to try to marry one of your dad’s lawyer buddies. I’m just saying that, as a parent, I want my daughter to have an easier time of it than I did. Cara and I had one of the quickest trips to success I’ve ever seen for writers, and I know how much we struggled to pay the rent at first. It was damn hard, and I don’t wish that on my child. That’s all I’m saying.” He threw up his hands. “The money I’ve made will make it easier on Vi—and Cara left behind a very decent inheritance for her—but that’ll pay bills. It’s not her achievement. My little girl’s not going to be happy unless she’s successful in her own right. That’s something no one can guarantee. So, yeah, I worry. I support her choices and will do everything I can to give her a hand up, but that doesn’t mean I don’t have concerns. That’s the only way I sympathize with your parents’ point of view. Don’t put me in the same category as them."

"Why would you care what category I put you in?" She went to the sink to wash her hands, then smoothed back a few wisps on her braided hair.

He followed her and set his hands on her shoulders. "Because I like you, and I want you to like me. You just said you don't like your parental units."

"Nope, not much."

"I'm sorry if I brought up bad memories for you." He kissed the nape of her neck, and his warm breath rushed against her skin, making her shiver.

"Not all the memories of my parents are bad. Just most of them." She tried to conjure up some great ones. Nothing came to mind. Most of the good ones were closely intermixed with not so good ones. Sad, but true. "Thank God I had my older brother."

"Tate, right." Neil rested his head against the back of hers, slipping his arms around her waist. "He's a lawyer like your dad. So he fulfilled what they wanted in a child."

"He did, for a while. Until he couldn't. He left the family firm for a much lower key situation." She let herself relax back against him, enjoying the feel of being held. "If he hadn't, he'd have lost his wife. He definitely made the right choice on that one."

"I'm glad for him." He stroked his fingertips over the bare strip of skin between the bottom of her shirt and the top of her pants. "I try hard not to put my work above my daughter."

"I know." And she did. She'd seen evidence of it many times since they'd arrived. The fact that he was here at all was proof in and of itself. Robert Patton would never, ever have done that for his daughter. Neil Graves hadn't hesitated. "You're a great dad. I'm sorry if I made you think that I think otherwise. It was a stupid, kneejerk reaction."

He hugged her tighter. "I'm sorry you have a history that makes that kind of reaction normal."

"Me too."

For some reason, his words made tears well in her eyes. Workaholics scared her, and the fact that he was one made her want to run like hell. Her emotions were clearly involved with him and with his daughter. Her heart said *stick around*, her mind said *bolt*.

But it hit her that the one area in her life where she'd never managed to take a real risk was in the romance department. The men she'd dated before hadn't been true contenders for her heart—and they'd all deliberately been the antithesis of her father: flaky, artistic, maybe a little too clingy. Men whose attention was nice for a little while, but would drive her batty in the long run, men who she could never really fall for, men who didn't challenge her to grow as a person. She'd never gone out with anyone who made her take him seriously, because she'd been too afraid to commit to someone who took life and work so seriously she'd get stuck in her mother's world of being dead last on the priority list.

It was an ugly realization to know she'd been pretty gutless when it came to her love life, and she'd been lying to herself about it for years. So fixated on not ending up with her father's clone, she'd never even stopped to think about what she really wanted, rather than running blind from what she didn't want. And the closer she'd gotten to Neil, the more she'd had to fight the urge to flee.

He tempted her too much, especially when she wasn't sure he could give her what she needed in the long haul. He was serious in all the wrong ways, and the way her heart skipped a beat any time he walked in the room meant her feelings were very, very serious about him. But maybe he was too much of a risk for her.

However, the thought of letting him go, letting fear win again...no.

Just no.

She didn't know what to do, what was right, what was best for her, and Neil, and Violet. Hurting them was the last thing she'd ever want to do. They'd been through enough already, losing Cara, losing Neil's parents, all in the last decade.

He nibbled at the tendon that connected her neck to her shoulder, dragging her attention back to the present. His fingers had edged up the hem of her tank top, slowly heading toward her breasts. Heat prickled through her, spreading in waves. God, she could never get enough of this, of him and how he made her feel.

Desire that never seemed to be very far from the surface began to boil within her. "Since we're conveniently alone... Wanna do bad things?"

"Nope, I only want to do all the good things with you." He caught her earlobe between his teeth and tugged. At the same time, he rocked his hips into her backside, the solid length of his erection proving just how earnest he was.

She reached back and gripped the outsides of his thighs. "I think I'll require a demonstration to be convinced that all the good things are better than the bad things I had in mind."

He smiled against her skin. "I'd be happy to show you."

"**B**ack in the kitchen again." Neil pushed open the swinging door and let Laurel and Violet precede him.

His daughter grinned back at him. "It's fun here, especially when Gloria threatens to kill you guys."

"I like how descriptive she is too," Laurel agreed, glee in her expression as she strapped on an apron. "You could get ideas from her about how to do people in for your next book, Neil."

"My next seven books, you mean." He hooked his apron over his head, then tied Violet's at her waist before he secured his. "There've been a lot of...suggestions."

Laurel snorted and Vi snickered. His daughter managed a lofty look for the adults. "Well, she's never wanted to kill me."

"Probably because you always volunteer to serve on the buffet line, thus avoiding her wrath." Laurel nudged her arm. "Out of sight, out of mind."

"Don't be mad 'cuz I'm smart." Vi stuck her tongue out, but then morphed into guilelessly angelic in the blink of an eye as the chef came into view. "Got anything for me to take out yet, Gloria?"

"I loaded up for you." The older woman nodded to a metal multi-shelved cart laden with several large bowls covered in plastic wrap. Gloria pinned the teen with a quelling gaze. "Go slowly so you don't drop anything."

"I will, I promise." Vi was suitably solemn as she took hold of the handle on the cart.

The old woman's expression didn't ease, but it rarely did. "Ruth's on the phone with her mom and dad, but then she'll be along to help you."

"Great." Vi moved toward the door to the dining room. "I'll try to keep her from running with the food."

"That'd take a miracle, but good luck," Gloria muttered as she used a dishcloth to dab at the sweat on her forehead. Her gaze fell on Laurel and Neil. "What are the two of you standing around for? Do I have to chase you around with a cleaver to make you work?"

"No, ma'am." Neil put on the same solemn mien as his daughter. Hey, she'd learned it from someone.

Laurel ducked away, and he could hear her smothering giggles as she scurried to the board where assignments were listed. They were both slated to work on different side dishes, so they went to one table in the kitchen to prep the ingredients.

It had been nice to find that they were on the same kitchen shift. Then again, he wasn't entirely certain Gloria hadn't shuffled things around a little to make that happen. She'd never confess it if she had though. But she was a lot nicer than she'd ever admit, cleavers notwithstanding.

Laurel secured her long hair in a bun—one of the chef's many rules. Then she checked the card for the recipe she was working on. "Hey, I haven't burned a thing and it's been—what?—three weeks now? Despite the death threats, The Woman of Many Knives is a really good teacher. I've made macaroni salad, au gratin potatoes, rice pilaf, and peach cobbler. Seriously, I made peach cobbler. All by myself. If she'll let me make a main dish, I might be able to invite people over for more than a potluck or catered dinner."

"Catering, huh?" Though Neil was stuck on her first sentence. Three weeks. They were almost a third of the way through the program. Time flew when you were having fun. And on deadline.

"Yeah, catering. I grew up with a silver spoon in my mouth, Graves." She shrugged and started peeling a small mountain of apples. "I know how to manage the help—Mother made certain."

"Trust fund baby," he teased with a mock-sneer, moving to a sink to rinse a boatload of cherry tomatoes. Cooking for crowds was a whole different way of thinking about food preparation.

Her smile faded a little. "People will say the same about Violet, so don't be a reverse snob about people like us. We don't choose to be born to parents with money."

"Point taken." He thought about that as he washed, how parental income affected kids. He'd grown up lower middle class—never quite enough money to go around, but he'd had everything he needed. And he'd been loved, which was more important than any amount of money. It hurt his heart to know that a young Laurel had had a life so lacking in love and acceptance. "Vi wanting to be an author with two parents who were successful novelists is going to result in comments too, huh?"

"Riding the coattails." Laurel made a sympathetic face. "But she'll prove them wrong, because she's awesome."

"Thanks." Pride suffused him, and also gratitude that this woman was so encouraging of his daughter. He didn't know what he'd done to deserve her, but he wasn't about to question his good fortune. Everything seemed a little better, a little easier to deal with when Laurel was around. Violet and he had laughed more in the last month than they had in the last twelve months combined, and part of that was Laurel's influence. She was funny and sarcastic and didn't take herself or anyone else too seriously. Not that she was a flake, but she didn't have an aneurysm over every little thing either.

There was a lesson in that for him, he knew. He'd tended to take everything too seriously.

"Don't thank me for the truth." She carefully cored and sliced the apples, her brow creased as she concentrated. Cooking didn't come naturally to her, but she made a real effort because it was part of the program. She'd signed on with The Enclave, so she didn't shirk the responsibilities that came with it. He liked that about her, the dichotomy of carefree and conscientious.

He brought his tomatoes back to the cutting board and started slicing them in half. After this he had to cut up some basil and feta cheese. This was going to be a pretty tasty salad. He glanced over to see Laurel cleaning up the apple cores. "I've been meaning to ask. How's your apprentice? I haven't even seen him, and he wasn't that late for the start of the program."

"Anti-social is too mild a word for him." She shrugged. "He's basically a hermit. He spent thirty years in IT, retired, and decided to pursue his secret passion for painting. His work is good, but I'm pretty sure he's subsisting on Cheetos in his cabin so he doesn't have to mingle with others in the dining room."

"He has to do his stint in the kitchen with other people." He motioned to the half-dozen other artists in the room.

She shook her head. "He has so many food allergies and sensitivities, he got a doctor's note saying he can't even be in an area where about fifty kinds of foods are present."

"Dang. A doctor's note." Neil snapped his fingers. "I should have thought of that."

Her eyes widened. "But then you'd get to spend less time with me."

"True." He bent to kiss the tip of her nose. "That would be tragic."

"Good answer." Her gaze dropped to his lips, as if daring him to do more, despite their audience. He resisted. Barely.

His voice was rougher than he intended when he replied, "I do what I can."

"I like what you can do."

She gave him a bright smile, and it warmed a place deep inside him that had been cold and barren for far too long. But he didn't like to think about what had turned him into an overly-serious ulcer candidate. It hadn't just been his divorce, or losing his parents, or even his ex dying. No, there was one moment, one day that had ripped the joy out of him for years. He'd done his best to put it behind him, for Violet and Cara's sakes, but some wounds never really healed, did they? He shook off the memories. It was a long time ago, and he was tired of dwelling on the past. Doing so never helped.

Laurel and he settled into companionable silence, working side by side. He liked how her arm or hip would bump into his occasionally. There was the thrill of sexual awareness, of course, but it was more than that. It felt like a real relationship, a partnership, or the start of one. But that wasn't quite true, was it? Sure, they were "dating," but she'd never spent the night in his cabin when Vi was there.

It was ironic. Laurel was the first thing to make him feel like the weight he carried wasn't going to crush him. She reminded him what it was like to want someone so intensely it burned. She reminded him that he was not only a father, novelist, or screenplay writer—he was a man, and it had been a very long while since he let himself be just a man. The fame and fortune he'd built meant he'd had more than his fair share of starlets and groupies wanting to scratch any carnal itches he might have had, and he enjoyed the short flings they offered, but that was all they were. Short-term and complication-free. That'd been his specialty since his divorce. He hadn't had energy or time for more.

Laurel offered him the same kind of uncomplicated arrangement for the summer, but with her...the feelings were more intense, the desire raged hotter, and he wasn't entirely sure he wanted this fling to be short-lived. Sadly, there was absolutely no way his stressed, insane existence would ever meld with her free-spirited, rootless lifestyle. He had a kid, so he could never bounce from coast to coast—or continent to continent—the way Laurel did. It was cringe-worthy to admit it, but he didn't have much to offer a woman like her. Great sex, sure, but what else? She didn't need his money, didn't give a damn about his fame, and wouldn't enjoy the constant juggling act he had to do to manage his competing priorities.

Where did that leave him? Nowhere. So he'd better enjoy whatever she was willing to give him. He had a feeling it was going to suck to lose her when their stay in Colorado ended. But he was a big boy. He'd suffered through all kinds of loss before, and he could do it again.

He hoped.

But he had to brace himself for when that finale came and be careful to protect his daughter as best he could. Because it looked like Vi might be falling in love with Laurel as much as Neil was.

CHAPTER SEVEN

He was in hell.

That was all Neil could think. *Hell*. Somehow, someway, he'd pissed off the universe and now he was being punished. He sat on the couch and stared at the letter from his editor, feeling his gut churn. Just reading it again made sweat pop out along his hairline. He swiped at it roughly, wanting nothing more than to burn the offending piece of paper and pretend he'd never seen it. He couldn't do this. He could not write any of this. Just thinking about how to rip his book apart the way his editor wanted made his mind gibber with panic. And made memories he wished he didn't have resurface to mock him.

"You look stressed." Laurel stood just inside the screen door, her head cocked as she studied him. Somehow he hadn't even noticed that she'd come in. "More stressed than usual, I mean. What's wrong?"

Yeah, as if he wanted to tell her about this. "Nothing, just busy."

"You're lying." Her tone was deceptively mild, but he knew her well enough now to understand when she was annoyed with him. She folded her arms. "If you don't want to talk to me, that's fine, but don't lie."

"You're right, I'm sorry." And he meant it. His crappy day shouldn't roll downhill onto her.

"Forgiven." A little smile tilted up one corner of her lips. She nodded to the coffee table that held his laptop and papers. "I'll leave you to it."

Leave him alone with this horrible letter? This thing that might actually drive him mad? Nausea roiled in his belly. He held out a hand before she could turn away. "Wait."

Her grin widened, and she came over to perch on the arm of the sofa. "So. What's wrong?"

"I'm blocked." There. That was a simple way to put it, without going into details that would give him nightmares.

She looked puzzled for a moment. "Uh...like you need a laxative?"

He snorted. "That would actually be easier to deal with. No, I have writer's block."

"Got it." Her look was sympathetic, her tone gentle. "Well, it happens to a lot of artists. You must have dealt with it before."

"Not like this."

She nodded as if she understood, but she didn't. She couldn't. "So, the screenplay isn't going well?"

"Not the screenplay."

"Then what?" She ticked off his projects on her fingers. "You turned in the story Violet was doing copy edits on, you turned in the novel. Do you have another project you're working on?"

"My editor sent back revisions on the novel." He pressed his thumbs against his temples and massaged, but it didn't relieve his tension.

"Oh. What does he—or she—want you to do that's blocking you?"

And relive the worst day of his life? Christ. He swallowed and closed his eyes. "It's just wrapped up in some seriously bad memories."

"Okay." Her expression went from kind to concerned. "Something to do with your parents, your ex-wife, other traumatic experiences that you haven't told me about yet?"

"The second two."

"Talking about it might help." She reached over and caught his hand, squeezing tight. "With the block and with making this something that doesn't block you anymore."

Yeah, right. His laugh was an ugly sound, even to his own ears. "I wish that was true, but some things will mess you up so badly that you never really get over them."

"And this is one of those things."

It wasn't a question, but he answered it anyway.

"Yeah," he sighed. "This is one of those things."

"How can I help?" She leaned closer, her dark eyes reflecting how much she cared about him. So sweet, so giving.

And he still couldn't tell her. Or rather, he didn't want to. So, it was time to change the subject. He used her hold on his hand to reel her in and tumble her into his lap. "Kiss it and make it better?"

She shifted to straddle his thighs and smirked down at him. "You want distraction rather than actual help?"

"Sometimes a distraction does help." He offered what he hoped was a convincing smile. "Your subconscious can work on the problem while you're busy with something else."

"Uh-huh." Skepticism oozed from her tone. "How many girls have gone for that line?"

Ha. As if he would fall into that trap. He let his smile widen. "You're the first I've tried it on, so I'm hoping I get a one hundred percent response rate."

"Right answer." She brushed her lips over his. "Condom?"

"In my nightstand." Because he shared the medicine cabinet with his teenage daughter. Yeah, he wanted to have that discussion.

She shimmied backward and pushed to her feet. "Well, come on."

Thank God. He felt the kind of intense relief that should be reserved for a man given a reprieve from the gallows. He rose and took her hand, bringing it to his lips to kiss. Then he led her into the bedroom, leaving the damn letter behind.

She turned toward him, her mouth open to speak, but he didn't let her get a word out, too afraid that she'd change her mind. So he hauled her against him, smothering whatever she might have said with his mouth. He plunged his tongue between her lips, kissing her hard, demanding a response. She moaned, clutching at his shoulders, her ardor quickly rising to match his. He loved the way she always reacted for him, and he needed that now more than ever, needed to forget, needed the bliss he found when he lost himself in her body.

He slid his hands down her back, grabbing the edge of her shirt. He broke the kiss just long enough to yank the garment over her head. "I want you, Laurel. I want you naked, I want to fuck you until I can't even remember my own name."

"I—"

His lips met hers again, cutting off her words. He honed in on her chest, stroking her through the soft lace of her bra, stimulating her nipples with the fabric. She whimpered and reached for the front of his jeans, fighting with the zipper while he toyed with her breasts. She opened his fly, then tugged at his tucked-in polo. They struggled to undress each other between kisses, their breathing harsh, their movements rushed.

God, he needed to be inside her. He dragged her over to the nightstand, scrambled for the condom, donning the rubber in record time.

Then he had her in his arms again, his mouth on hers, backing her against the nearest wall. She wrapped her legs around his waist, and he shoved deep in one sharp, swift thrust.

Oh, yeah.

Nothing, nothing ever felt as good as sliding deep into a wet, willing woman. Her hot sex clenching tight around his shaft. It was, hands down, the most visceral experience in the world.

And with Laurel, it was better than it had been...maybe ever.

Clamping his hands on her perfect ass, he rode her into the wall. It was hard and wild and rough and he couldn't stop if someone had a gun to his head. Her fingers gripped his hair so tightly it stung, and her other hand was busy raking down his arm. "Yes, Neil. Yes. Right there, right there. Just like that."

"You're killing me." His hips pistoned, driving his shaft into her as fast as he possibly could, trying to forge their bodies into one.

Her chuckling was throaty, her voice hitching each time he pounded into her. "Can you think of a better way to go?"

"Not one."

Sweat made their flesh glide, and he felt his orgasm begin to boil up from his balls. He thrust deep, over and over and over again. Heat simmered in his blood, a fever he could never quench.

"I'm going to—" Her sentence ended in a long, low moan.

The feel of her channel fisting around his shaft was more than enough to catapult him over into climax. Hot jets of fluid spurted out of him, draining him of all thought, all emotion, all past and present. There was only this moment of exquisite ecstasy while he pumped into her sex.

And it was mind-blowingly perfect.

Her little sighs as she came down from the high made a smile curve his lips. Her fingers relaxed and she petted him. He held her close and eased them away from the wall. He took a few steps to the right and settled her on the mattress, slipping in behind her. He buried his face in the crook of her neck, breathing in the feminine scent of her, and let his mind drift. He let the air out of his lungs, and it took a moment to identify the sudden quiet well-being that enveloped him.

Even in the middle of madness, he found peace in her arms.

"So, did your block work itself out subconsciously?" Laurel propped herself up on her elbow and looked down at him. While the sex had been as marvelous as ever—if perhaps a little more frantic—now that she'd come down off the high, she couldn't put the stricken look on his face when she'd walked into the cabin out of her mind. "I know I'm good, but if it's something that scarred you for life, I may not be that good."

His eyes crinkled at the corners, and he ran a fingertip along her collarbone. "I feel like any response I make to that is going to come out wrong and piss you off."

"I'll take it that you'd still have problems doing your revisions." She kept her voice light. "That still leaves my suggestion."

"Talking it out." He appeared more than a little skeptical.

"I know, it's such a chick thing to say." She settled against him and rested her chin on his chest, but still held his gaze. "You said it had to do with your ex-wife and other trauma. Something related to the divorce?"

He was quiet long enough that she thought he might not answer. "It's what led to the divorce, more or less."

A memory tickled at the back of her mind, and she almost winced, but forced herself not to chicken out of this conversation. She had a feeling this was something he needed to talk about, whether he wanted to or not. She cleared her throat. "I seem to recall there was some scandal surrounding your breakup, but that was years ago and I don't really keep up with Hollywood gossip."

"Scandal." He snorted and shook his head. "The only scandal was one created by the paparazzi and a fame-hungry bitch."

That was probably the most unforgiving statement she'd ever heard him make. Not good. "The actress who starred in your first film, right? They turned your zombie apocalypse slasher trilogy into movies." She managed a smile. "Those scared me so bad I almost peed my pants. It was awesome."

He chuckled, slipping his fingers into her hair. "You're welcome."

When no further details were forthcoming, she prodded, "So, you didn't hook up with the starlet?"

"No," he growled. "I never cheated on my wife. Our marriage was on the rocks well before any media-created scandals."

"Why?"

A huge rush of air escaped his lungs, the sound both tired and sad. "I'd like to say we just grew apart. We were college sweethearts, pregnant with a kid before we'd even graduated, and the book business isn't exactly low pressure."

"Right, you both sold your first novels right out of college." Violet had filled Laurel in on that little tidbit.

"We both got three-book deals within a month of each other. We'd both majored in creative writing, so it was what we'd gone to school for, and it was better than flipping burgers." He shrugged, his gaze focusing on the ceiling. "We had to find a way to pay the bills. Kids aren't cheap."

"So I've heard." This time, she waited him out. She was immune to the silent treatment—her mother was a master at it. Neil was a rank amateur in comparison. A few minutes passed, but he grunted and finally gave in.

"Cara and I were both only children, and we'd always wished we had siblings. Neither of us wanted just one kid." A smile twitched on and off his face. "We'd worked hard to build our careers. Cara racked up two more book deals with other publishers, and I made the *New York Times* bestseller list. Things were right on track and our lives were...perfect. So, when Vi was maybe four or five we decided it was time to have another baby."

"Did you have fertility issues?" Laurel had known her fair share of couples who'd hit rocky patches because of infertility.

"No, Cara got pregnant within six months of stopping birth control."

The raw pain in his voice told her what was coming, and hot sympathy squeezed her chest.

"She was in her third trimester, and we were ready for the baby to come. The nursery was decorated, I had the bag packed for the hospital...we were so damn excited." His Adam's apple bobbed as he swallowed hard. "She was a little worried because she hadn't felt the baby move in a while, so we went in to see the doctor. We found out our son was stillborn."

"Oh my God." She wrapped an arm around his waist, hugging him close. This was why he'd tensed up when Vi had mentioned siblings, because they'd lost a child. "Neil."

"She still had to go through full childbirth. They induced labor, and even though we knew she'd deliver a dead baby, somehow going through the motions made the whole thing so much worse." His voice cracked with emotion, and he pinched the bridge of his nose. Laurel just held him while he struggled to regain his composure. "She sank into postpartum depression and just...shut me out. At first, I tried to give her space. I was going through some heavy shit too and I didn't know how to deal with any of it. Both of us focused on Violet and buried ourselves in work. Cara slowly pulled out of the depression, but somehow she and I never really reconnected. It was like she couldn't even look at me without thinking about the son we lost. I tried everything I could think of...counseling, romantic getaways, anything to save our marriage." A muscle twitched in his cheek, and he looked for all the world as if he were going to cry. "Nothing really worked. She was just done with me, with us."

Tears burned the back of Laurel's eyes. "I'm so sorry, Neil."

He pushed himself upright and continued talking. The floodgates had opened and he seemed compelled to get it all out. "I started commuting back and forth to LA to work on the zombie movies, got tired of dealing with hotels so I bought a condo to use whenever I was there, and Cara was more than happy for me to stay away as long as I wanted. She didn't want me to come home, and if it weren't for Violet, I probably wouldn't have. Finally, she suggested we call it quits." He glanced at Laurel when she sat up and scooted next to him. He shook his head. "I hate to admit how huge a relief that was, like we'd been trapped in this hellish limbo since the baby, and even though the outcome was awful, at least it was done and I could move on."

She looped her arm through his, craving the contact, and not wanting him to withdraw. "So how did the starlet come into it?"

"Hell, I don't even know." He forked his fingers through his hair, gripping the long strands. "She'd thrown herself at me at every script reading we did, but it was clear she saw me as some kind of trophy, and I didn't have a single ounce of energy left to deal with her ego. I turned her down and I wasn't nice about it. I was married, you know? What the hell?"

Considering her parents didn't believe in fidelity, his answer was more than a little heartening. She squeezed his biceps. "With your relationship crumbling, I'm guessing most people would have understood you turning to someone else for comfort."

One hand made a slicing motion through the air. "Good for them, I wouldn't have understood. I took vows, damn it, and I meant them. Until the judge signed off on the divorce, I was still married."

"But the actress was pissed about your rejection and told the media you had sex with her anyway." Her voice hardened, angry on his behalf. What a nightmare, and some woman's bruised pride had made a terrible time in his life so much worse.

"That sums it up, yeah. Cara and I had already filed for the divorce by the time the fabricated story broke, but the press decided I was a cheating sleaze and my wife had left me for it." He drew up a knee and propped his elbow on it. "No one gave a damn that it wasn't true, even though Cara and I released a joint statement that contradicted what was being reported."

Because news ran on sex and violence, and some guy's innocence wasn't sexy enough to merit mention. He was guilty, end of story. He tugged his arm away and slipped it around her waist. She laid her head against his shoulder. "So...crappiest year of your life?"

"I might have to slit my wrists if I ever have a worse one." His tone was so matter-of-fact, it took her a moment to process what he'd said. "Wow."

He dragged a palm down his face. "So...that's why I'm blocked. I had a character get pregnant at the end of the last book."

She bludgeoned her mind to remember which one was his last book. She liked his work, but wasn't so big a fan that she read every novel the second it came out, and didn't always read them in the order they were released. A pregnant character...then it clicked. "Right, the school teacher turned serial killer's girlfriend."

"Yep. My editor wants her to have a miscarriage." The words were utterly bleak. "She thinks it will up the emotional stakes and make the serial killer's spiral out of control more relatable to the reader."

"Oh fuck me." That was all she could think to say.

He huffed out a laugh, squeezed her tight, and kissed her forehead. "Yeah. That."

They remained there in silence for a few minutes, and she tried to think of what she could say or do that might help. All she had was tough practicality to offer, and she hoped it wouldn't annoy him. Scooting around meant she could face him, but she stayed close enough that her knees touched his legs.

"Okay, I want you to think about what your editor suggested." She held up her hand when he opened his mouth to reply. "Not about the inner freak out you'd have over dredging up those emotions. I want the opinion of the seasoned writer who has skin thicker than a rhinoceros when it comes to taking criticism about his work. Would what your editor suggested really make the story better? If not, see if you can talk her out of it."

He nodded, his mouth tight. "I think...that's part of the problem. As soon as I read it, I knew she was right. Then the reality of what it would take to write it hit hard, the personal cost to the man, not the author. And I know the author side of me needs to win this one, but... Jesus. How?"

The torment in his gaze made her heart break, but if she was going to really help him through this, she had to get him to keep it in perspective. "I had this class in college where the professor made people draw a slip of paper from a basket on his desk. Each slip had an emotion on it, and we had to paint that emotion in any way we saw fit. That was our final project. Of course, I got inadequacy."

"You're amazing. I can't imagine you ever being inadequate." He paused and she saw the moment the lightbulb went on. "Ah. Your parents."

"Yeah, good old Mommy and Daddy who hated that they ended up with an artist in their lawyerly midst, and never failed to make sure I knew it." She loved the anger that fired in his gaze, pissed that her parents could be so unwilling to accept her. She appreciated the sentiment. "I've gotten over it when it comes to my work, but when my heart is involved, when I'm vulnerable to a person, there's still that little voice in the back of my head telling me I'm not good enough, that something is wrong with me because I'm so different from my entire family, that I'll never belong anywhere, that I don't deserve to because I couldn't conform, because I'm a square peg who wouldn't trim herself down to fit in that round hole. Every other Patton managed to, so why couldn't I?"

The anger burned even brighter, and he linked his fingers with hers. "I'm glad you didn't."

"Me too." She patted his thigh. "But I had to rip open all those old wounds and pour what I felt into that painting."

He cringed a bit. "Let me guess—it's one of your best pieces?"

"I have no idea. As soon as I got my passing grade for the class, I burned the canvas." She shrugged at his shocked look. "Sorry, honey, I'm not here to moralize. The bottom line is I never, ever wanted to see that piece again and be reminded of all the things I'd never be, of all the memories I'd never really get rid of or bury deep enough I'd forget them. I imagine once you've made it through all the revisions and edits, you'll probably feel the same and never read that particular book again."

"Yeah." Pained resignation settled over his face. "Vi's not going to be doing the copy edits on that one. She knows what happened, and she'd have no problem figuring out that was an accounting of what I went through. Minus the killing spree."

"Good thing too." She rubbed her thumb over his palm, trying to give him comfort where there really was none. "Some things just suck and are always going to suck. But you do get through them."

His mouth opened, but nothing came out. He clamped it shut and swallowed. "Will...will you stay with me while I do the revisions?"

"If you need me to, yes." She recognized what it would have taken a workaholic like him to admit he needed help to get his work done. Keeping her voice as casual as possible, she added, "You can bring your laptop over to my cabin when I'm painting, and I can come here if I'm just visualizing or sketching."

"Thank you," he croaked. "I think it would help to have someone nearby who understands how hard this is and why."

"I'll be here if you need a sanity check, Graves."

Something shifted in his expression, but she couldn't quite pinpoint what. He tugged her forward and kissed her. The brush of his lips was lighter than a butterfly's wing, and yet made her heart clench. He pressed her back on the bed, insinuating his big body between her thighs. He didn't enter her immediately, just mated his mouth with hers.

Their lovemaking was unhurried and very, very thorough. Time stretched and became elastic, the only thing that mattered in the world was Neil and the ecstasy he brought her. She climaxed so many times, she lost count. He seemed intent on touching, stroking, and kissing every single inch of her body. It was one of the few times their joining hadn't been rushed or desperate. This was a slow worship. Sweat slipped in slow beads down their skin, their limbs tangled, sensation piled on top of sensation, every moment bringing more pleasure.

As a thank you present for being a decent human being, she couldn't complain.

CHAPTER EIGHT

L aurel's feet were cold.

She could find socks, but then she'd have to get up from her comfortable spot on Neil's couch. By straightening her legs slightly, she could tuck her feet under his thigh. Lovely. She wiggled her toes, and grinned when he cast her glance. He winked and refocused on his laptop. He'd finished everything except his screenplay, so his stress level had come down a bit in the last couple of weeks. It had been really nice to see.

With her feet warming up, she could concentrate on the sketchbook propped on her bent knees. She was finishing up a drawing of a lark. It was a plain, rather ugly little bird, but she'd liked its song and one had hopped around through tree branches looking at her curiously that morning. So, by the time she was done with it, using her signature Laurel Patton color magic, it was going to be a gorgeous sight to behold. The way its song made her feel was going to end up on the canvas and translate those drab feathers into brilliant plumage.

"Hey, Laurel, you said your nephew's birthday is in August. Are his parents having a party?" Violet perched at the small desk in the corner of the living room—her usual spot every evening when they got in a last bit of work after dinner. Tonight, she was editing a chapter of her novel based on some of Laurel's feedback.

"Of course." She arched her eyebrows. "We need pictures of him smeared in cake to appropriately humiliate him when he goes on his first date."

"Oh, is that what we're supposed to do when our children go on their first date?" Neil looked up, a truly maniacal smile on his face.

"Don't you dare!" Vi launched a pen across the room at him, hitting him in the knee. Neil looked like he was going to throw the pen back, but Laurel grabbed it from him.

"I could always go with the tried-and-true threatening approach and make the guy wet his pants." The evil grin on his face widened. "I'll take a page from Gloria's book and just sit there sharpening all the kitchen knives with a stack of reference books beside me on how to dispose of dead bodies."

"Um, Dad?" Instead of shooting back a sarcastic remark, Violet bit her lower lip. "While I've been working on the romance part of my book, I realized…"

Laurel held her breath, suspecting that she knew what was coming, but wasn't sure if Neil had the same suspicions.

But he nodded easily, his smile gentling into one of understanding. "You realized it might not be just your heroine who likes boys *and* girls? And that your first date might not being with a guy?"

Vi eyes went round. "You knew?"

The breath eased out of Laurel, and she stayed quiet to see how this played out. She was glad Violet felt comfortable having this conversation with her there.

Setting his laptop aside, he leaned toward his daughter. "Honey, I read your drafts. *And* I know that authors often work through their personal issues in their writing."

Laurel tried not to cringe at that, reminded of the godawful revisions he'd had to deal with this summer and the personal hell it put him through.

The teen nodded sagely. "It's cheaper than therapy."

Snorting, he reached out a hand and Violet rose to take it. She squeaked when he hauled her onto his lap and wrapped her in a bear hug. "I love you, baby girl. I don't care who you date—guys, girls, non-binary—as long as they treat you well."

"I never doubted that. For real." Her gray gaze met her father's, her expression serious. She stretched out her legs and her feet tangled with Laurel's. Those gray eyes swung toward her and Laurel offered the teen a small smile, catching the girl's ankle and giving it a supportive squeeze. Vi pulled in a breath and looked up at Neil. "I just, like, thought you'd want to know before I brought a girlfriend home."

He frowned down at her as if something had just occurred to him. "This isn't you confessing that you and Ruth—"

"OMG, Dad, no!" Violet's nose wrinkled in horror. "We're girlfriends, but not like *girlfriend* girlfriends. Ruth is way too tomboy for me."

The look on her face made Laurel have to work to hold back a grin. "So, if you're going to like a girl, it's going to be a girly-girl?"

Amusement crinkled the corners of Neil's eyes. "You want to date the prom queen someday."

Vi's grin was cheeky. "I want to be the prom queen's gay awakening."

And that was when Laurel lost it completely, curving an arm around her middle as she laughed until her sides ached. Violet dissolved into giggles, and Neil fought against laughter for about ten seconds before the hilarity won out. After a few minutes the three of them were leaning against each other, trying to get a grip on their guffaws. Once one of them got themselves under control, another would start chuckling and it would set the others off.

"Okay, let's pull ourselves together." Laurel wiped the tears from her eyes, trying to remember what they'd been talking about before the gay awakening. Right, toddlers smeared in cake. "Why were you asking about my nephew's birthday?"

"Well, August isn't that far away." The teen shrugged, pushing to her feet and moving across the room to sit at her desk again. "If his birthday is early in the month, you're going to miss his party."

"No, he was born at the end of August. I'm headed to my brother's place for the party right after the program ends."

Neil let out a breath. "Wow, we're at the halfway mark."

A pool of silence engulfed the room, their laughter evaporating like it never existed, and Laurel was sure she wasn't the only one not looking forward to the end of summer. Her reasons might be different from theirs, but this program had been Halcyon days for almost everyone here. Mimi had mentioned that the dynamic of the group for this round of the program was the best she'd ever seen, and she was going to be sad when everybody left. Laurel suspected the younger woman would most miss having her favorite famous horror writer in residence, but she had no doubt Mimi was right about this group. Some great projects were going to come out of this summer from both the mentors and apprentices. There was just that kind of magic in the air. Like everyone was at the top of their game, and the energy here fed the creativity.

At first, Laurel had assumed it was just how all programs at The En-clave started, then people settled in for the long haul. But it had never worn off. She was going to have five new canvases either complete or mostly done by the time the summer ended. That never happened because she always wanted to keep tweaking her work, never quite satisfied with the results. This time? She was pretty damn happy with the final products. She couldn't even remember the last time she was so pleased with what she'd accomplished.

"Halfway." Violet looked stricken, and for a moment, Laurel thought the girl might cry. She whipped around to face the desk, tension vibrating from her.

The intense reaction made Laurel frown. "You okay, sweetie?"

After a few deep breaths that made her thin shoulders rise and fall, the teen turned back and smiled. "Fine. It's just going to suck to go back to LA. I like it here."

Her face was too pale and that grin was faked, Laurel was sure of it. But since she choked up a little whenever she thought about leaving, she couldn't blame the girl.

"I like it here too," Neil said quietly. "I'm going to miss everyone."

"Do you think we'll see any of them again?" Violet's eyes were wide and pleading. "Can we have a reunion here next summer?"

"I don't think The Enclave works that way," Laurel replied as gently as she could. "Though there's no reason we can't all keep in touch and try to visit when we can. Ruth and her parents are in Seattle, Helen and Pedro are in Austin. It wouldn't be that hard to get to those places, especially if your dad's going on a book tour."

He nodded. "Next year, for the book I just finished revisions on."

Right. The novel of pain and suffering. Then again, he was a horror writer, so technically all of his novels featured suffering of one kind or another, but this had been a much more personal kind of pain. She'd been with him for every moment of those revisions, had rubbed his back and held his hair back the time he'd gone into the bathroom to heave his guts up.

As not-fun as that had been, it was good to feel needed. She hadn't experienced that much in her life, especially with family. Tate had been the golden boy until long after he'd moved out of the house, so she'd always needed him far more than he'd needed her. She was used to being superfluous. Sure, she had friends scattered across the globe from all her travels, but she wasn't essential to their lives. With Neil and Violet, she felt like she offered something they didn't have. And not just because Cara wasn't around—Laurel would have befriended the Graveses no matter what. She would have cared about them no matter who else was part of their lives.

She doubted anything would have stopped her from loving them.

The truth of that hit her hard.

She loved them. Individually and together as a family. But what could she do about it? This summer was an ephemeral thing. She'd remain friends with Violet, but Neil? He could cut her off and that would be that. They'd agreed from the beginning that this affair/mini-relationship was only for the length of the program. A knot formed in her belly at the thought, but it was all too true. He hadn't mentioned anything about a future together, and she didn't know if she could be the one to reach out. That old, ugly sense of inadequacy still plagued her.

What if he—like so many before him—thought she wasn't good enough to keep around?

She stared into space for a long time, trying to sort out all her thoughts and feelings. It wasn't until Neil set his laptop down on the coffee table with a clatter that she snapped back to the present. The sun had long gone down, and it was pitch black outside. On any normal day, she'd have headed back to her cabin by now.

Violet rose and stretched. "You know, it's okay for you to sleep over.

You guys have been dating for six weeks. I took health class and I watch TV, so it's not like I don't know what you guys are doing when I'm hanging out with Ruth or babysitting the twins."

"Um…" Laurel had no quick-witted response to that one.

Neil smirked. "Told ya."

"Yeah, because that's the kind of comment that might get you laid tonight." Then she closed her eyes and pressed her fingers to her lids while the Graveses laughed. "You two are pains in the butt, you know that right?"

"It's part of our charm," he assured her.

She shot him an incredulous look. "Is that what you call it? Charm?"

"Of course," they answered at the same time, both looking a bit wounded.

"I'm going to go brush my teeth. You guys have fun. Try not to get too loud tonight." With that, Vi wandered into the bathroom and closed the door.

"I think your daughter just traumatized me for life." Laurel set aside her sketchbook while Neil snickered and offered her a hand up.

"Kids will do that on a fairly regular basis."

Because she really didn't want to be alone, staring at her ceiling and having her thoughts chase themselves in circles all night, she let him lead her into his bedroom. She'd resisted before now, maybe to protect Violet, maybe to protect herself. Both had been fruitless.

Yeah, she could use some distraction. And Neil was just the man for the job.

"Woohoo!"

Screeching at a pitch that would make dogs howl, Violet swung out on a rope over the lake. At the top of the arc, she let go, crashing into the water with a terrific splash. She came up laughing, slicking her hair back from her face. Ruth swam up and the two girls grabbed on to each other, chattering a million miles an hour.

The sun shone brightly, and Neil sat next to Laurel on a couple of folding chairs. He'd taken a rare day off from writing—okay, he'd gotten some in before Vi woke up—and he was enjoying some time outdoors soaking up the sunshine while the breeze ruffled his hair. He had a cold beer in one hand, and Laurel's slim palm nestled in the other. They'd swum for an hour before they'd gotten out to sit on the beach, but the teens were still going strong. He sighed, contentment winding through him. The feeling was weird, but he couldn't protest.

It was really nice to see Vi acting like a normal girl, less serious, less like the world rested on her narrow shoulders. She'd blossomed in a lot of ways the last couple of months, and he hoped this meant some of the grief over her mother's loss had gotten a little easier to bear.

This summer had been good for both of them. He'd somehow managed to meet all of his insane deadlines so far. Only the script draft remained unfinished, and he had a good handle on it. Even better, he'd had the amazing good fortune to meet Laurel. She'd been a godsend for both his daughter and him. He'd never have survived this program without her. He was starting to wonder how he'd survive life without her when it came time to part. But the truth was, his existence was a series of insane deadlines and jumping from one ulcer-inducing scenario to another. That was no kind of life to offer a woman like Laurel. She would hate it, and he would hate disappointing her.

"Let's race to shore!" Ruth shouted, splashing through the water as she tried to dart toward the beach.

Violet overtook her within a few yards, and led the rest of the way. She slogged out onto the rocky beach in front of the adults. Maybe ten seconds later, Ruth emerged behind her.

Raising her arms in triumph, Vi danced in a little circle. "I win, I win!"

"Only because we're in the water." Ruth propped her fists on her hips and grinned. "Let's put some running shoes on and see who wins."

"I'm not that dumb." Vi squeezed the water out of her wet hair. "I'd totally lose."

"You seem to be enjoying all the swimming this summer," Neil commented. "Maybe you can look at joining the swim team at school."

"No!" Her face set into mulish lines as she faced him. "I'm so not interested. At all."

"Okay." He shrugged, uncertain where the sudden drama had come from. "No need to bite my head off."

"Sorry." But her tone suggested otherwise. She waded back into the lake, and paddled away from shore, striking out for open water.

"Don't go too far out, please!" he called.

She shot a resentful look over her shoulder. "I won't!"

Ruth stood there looking puzzled, but then followed her friend.

When the girls were out of earshot, Laurel whispered, "Whoa, someone's in a mood."

"It's not the first time lately." Neil shook his head. "She's been in a snit for almost a week. There was a gigantic meltdown yesterday morning about—"

"Hey, Laurel! Hey, Neil!" A trio of other artists broke from the treeline, loaded down with towels and six packs of Pepsi or Pabst Blue Ribbon.

And that was the end of any serious conversation. Neil crossed his ankles. "Looks like we're having a party."

He waved a welcome to the newcomers, while Laurel hopped up to greet everyone. He sat back and watched her socialize, enjoying the way her bikini clung to her curves. She had, bar none, the nicest ass he'd ever seen. Her quick laugh drew his attention back to the fact that they had company. She glanced over her shoulder, her smile inviting him to join in the inevitable fun. After pushing out of his chair, he went to do just that. As if he could resist the temptation she offered. He hadn't succeeded so far. But, then, he hadn't tried very hard, had he?

Damn, he was going to miss her. Talking to her, laughing with her, watching her paint, making love with her. He tried not to think about the fact that the three months had somehow dwindled down to a handful of weeks. Were they down to five weeks? Maybe it was four. The time slipped away in a lovely haze here, where the days blurred into each other.

So, the only thing he could do was make sure to savor every second he had left.

"I think this party is unauthorized." Mimi charged down the path, trying to look stern. Since she didn't have a stern bone in her body, everyone laughed. She giggled, turned, and beckoned to someone behind her.

A lanky guy in a delivery uniform stepped forward, appearing more than a little uncomfortable. He cleared his throat. "Which one of you is Neil Graves?"

"Here." Neil toasted the other man with his beer bottle.

"Sign, please." The lanky dude thrust a digital pad in Neil's direction, and he scrawled an illegible signature across it. After taking back the pad, the guy dug around in his messenger bag and handed over a large envelope. He nodded and pivoted to return the way he'd come. "I can find my way back."

"He said only you could sign, so I brought him out here. I saw you head this way a few hours ago, so I took a gamble you were still here." Mimi winked. "Plus, it was kinda fun to drag him over the river and through the woods. Literally."

"He looks so pleased to have gotten a taste of nature," Laurel quipped.

Mimi sucked in her cheeks, trying not to laugh. She choked out, "He stepped in a big pile of deer poop."

The group dissolved into guffaws, and Mimi stopped fighting the giggles.

Ignoring them, Neil walked over to his chair to sit while he opened the envelope. A short note from his agent was jotted on a Post-It stuck to the front of a thick contract. It took a while to read through the legalese, and he could feel the tension start to build in his neck and shoulders, as if the weight of the world just got a little heavier.

"Damn," he sighed, suddenly weary.

"What's wrong?" Laurel settled into her chair sideways, leaning over the armrest to look at what he held.

"Nothing's wrong." Because he should be thrilled about this news—as his agent had said in the note—but he wasn't. "You know my last trilogy? Not the new serial killer one, but—"

"The *Sinister* series?" she filled in. "Of course. Creepy as hell."

His lips twitched, but he couldn't quite manage a real smile. "One of the cable channels wants to make a TV show out of it."

"But you don't look happy." She leaned back in her seat, her gaze considering. "They want you to write scripts for it."

"Nailed it one guess." He tucked the contract into its holder. He'd have to read it more carefully later. "They even want to fly a rep here to talk to me about it."

"Tell them no," she burst out.

That brought his head up, and he stared at her. "What?"

Her lips pursed and she looked up at the cloudless blue sky, as if she didn't know how or what to say to him. She almost looked like she wanted to cry.

"Hey. Talk to me." He tapped his sandal against hers.

"You take on too much, Neil." Her tone was somewhere between exasperated and concerned. "Right now, you're managing to keep everything together, meet all your obligations, but how long will that last if you can't or won't say no to anyone?" She held up her hand like she wanted to ward off any response he had. "You told me once that Vi was your number one priority, and I believed you. But what's your number two priority? What's number three? You only have so many hours in a day—are you spending them on what's most important to you? If not, you need to either turn down some offers or farm them out."

He drummed his fingers on the armrest. "It's so ingrained when you're a struggling writer, not to say no to any good opportunity. What if that chance never comes up again? What if you said no to the thing that would launch you into superstardom?"

"Newsflash, Graves." She swatted his knee. "You're already a superstar. Do you need more money?"

"No. Having Violet right out of college meant I never got to have the chance to be reckless and crazy with my money like most people who experience early success. Everything went to making sure she had what she needed, then to making sure she had college paid for, then to making sure I had retirement set aside so she wasn't stuck taking care of me when I'm too old to work. Every dime of my royalties has gone to savings or investments." He paused. "Okay, I have a classic Mustang convertible too. One toy's not too much."

"Well, you no longer have to say yes. Or if you say yes, it can be on your terms." She swung her arm in an expansive arc. "Let them make the TV show and pay you handsomely for it, but maybe recommend another writer. It's okay to delegate."

"You're rocking my world with your wild and stress-free ideas," he drawled. And he'd honestly never considered turning over his work for someone else to mess with. When he wrote the script, he had at least some control in how his novels translated to the big screen.

But what if he could maintain some creative oversight without being involved in the day-to-day operation of the television show? All he had to do was tell his agent he wanted to renegotiate the contract terms. The man made a good amount of cash from his percentage of Neil's earnings—it was okay to make him earn it.

"You're thinking about it. Good, keep doing that because I'm totally right." Laurel patted his wrist. "I'm going to swim some more."

She hopped up, kissed him with lingering sweetness, and went to join Vi and Ruth in the water. He settled deeper into his seat and took a swig of beer, considering how he might make this TV gig work.

And he already felt better just realizing he wouldn't be burdened with one more good thing. "Huh."

CHAPTER NINE

"We only have a week left, baby." Neil poked his head into Violet's room, taking in the piles of stones of various shapes and sizes that seemed to have grown exponentially in the months they'd been here. "You may want to start weeding out your collection and decide which ones will come with us and which will be released back into the wild."

She threw herself in front of him, clamping her hands on each side of the doorframe to block his way. "They're all coming back with me."

"Vi, that's crazy." Shaking his head, he stepped back. "What are you going to do with all of these rocks?"

"If they don't go back to LA, I don't go back to LA," she snapped as she rushed by him and flounced out of the house, slamming the screen door behind her.

He projected his voice so he knew she heard him. "Violet Marie, this discussion is not finished."

"I have to babysit now," she yelled without turning around. "I'll be back later. Then you can finish ruining my life."

Neil swore under his breath. These outbursts had become more frequent in the last couple of weeks. The closer they got to the end of summer, the moodier she'd become. She was more prone to lash out over little things and had had a few epic meltdowns. He was uncertain if this was just a part of being a teenager, or if something direr was wrong. Should he confront her about her attitude or let it blow over?

If he were brutally honest, he'd admit he was avoiding that argument. He feared her explosions might have something to do with his deepening relationship with Laurel—this was the first time Vi had ever gotten to know someone he'd dated since he split up with her mother. He was scared to death he was going to have to choose between the two females in his life that meant the most to him, and he didn't want to face that.

Not yet.

He figured chasing her down and confronting her in front of Helen, her family, and probably Ruth, would only exacerbate the problem and make communication impossible, so he'd have to wait until she returned. Which was several hours from now.

Going over to Laurel's held some appeal, but he wasn't really in the mood for company. Frankly, he'd like a snifter of good scotch and a way to make all his problems evaporate for a while. Since that was unlikely to happen, he might as well try to write.

Try was the operative word.

Mostly it was a lesson in frustration of attempting to figure out what was up with Vi and what the hell he should do about this thing he had going on with Laurel. Ask her to date long-distance? See if she was available for a standing hook-up any time she happened to be in southern California? What would she want, if anything?

And how would their choices about the future affect his child? Would breaking things off with Laurel at the end of summer be better for Violet? She seemed to adore Laurel, but maybe she'd changed her mind and didn't know how to tell him. She'd been doing so well, been happy and carefree, but seemed to have regressed. Only instead of grief-stricken, now she was angry.

Yeah, it was definitely time to have a talk with his daughter. He hoped this was nothing more than a growing pain, but he had to know for sure.

For all of their sakes.

L aurel sat on her porch, ostensibly to sketch the mountains, but her paper was mostly filled with little doodles of Gloria and Ruth, Mateo and Jina, Neil and Violet. Those last two had the biggest drawings. She didn't want to forget any of the people she'd met here. It had been a golden summer, perfect in many ways. She wanted to capture it somehow so it couldn't escape her, so she wouldn't forget a single moment. Her heart squeezed at the thought of it ending.

A door slammed, and she looked up, startled.

Violet came storming up the dirt road, swiping at her cheeks.

After tossing her sketchbook aside, Laurel rose and held out her hand. "Hey, honey. Come here. What's up?"

Vi made a beeline for her, throwing herself into Laurel's arms and sobbing as if her heart might break. They sank down on the porch steps, and Laurel rocked the teen, stroking her hair and crooning reassurances. She had no idea what might be wrong, but whatever it was wasn't good.

"He's so mean sometimes," Vi choked out.

Eyebrows arching, Laurel asked, "Your dad?"

The girl nodded, her dark locks rustling against Laurel's shirt. "He won't let me take all the rocks Ruth and I collected. I just want something to remind me of here when we have to go back to that place."

The last word came out as a vicious snarl. "You mean LA?"

"I hate it there." A fresh round of sobs had Vi burrowing into Laurel's shirt.

Laurel blinked. "What's wrong with LA, sweetie? It's not just because you're in a new school, is it?"

"The school sucks. I have no friends. None. Not even one." Vi's voice hardened. "The teachers are even worse."

"All of the teachers?" Laurel leaned back to get a look at her face.

"Yes!" Her chin jutted mulishly. "The English teacher is the worst. He's an asshole."

Since Violet wasn't prone to swearing, Laurel's eyebrows arched in surprise. "What's he been doing?"

A million possibilities, each worse than the next, pelted through her mind. Had this man touched Vi? Teachers having affairs with students popped up on the news with alarming frequency these days. Cold dread knotted in Laurel's gut. *Oh God. Oh. God.* She didn't know how to handle this. She wasn't a parent. But if Vi felt comfortable telling her about it, she wouldn't silence her. So she sat and waited for the girl to speak, her palms slicked with sweat.

"You have to swear you won't tell my dad."

Crap. If anything, the knot in her belly grew tighter. "I promise. But, honey, you have to know if it's bad enough, I'd want you to tell your dad."

Vi's shoulder jerked in a shrug. "My teacher's just...he makes fun of my writing. Because the famous Neil Graves is my father. He caught me writing part of my book in his class—I was done with the assignment!" A tear streaked down her cheek. "And he made me read it to the whole class, then he went on and on about how we had a budding novelist on our hands, only he said it in a mean way, and the whole class laughed at me."

"Wow, what a dick." Okay, it was bad, but not as bad as Laurel had feared. She didn't know if she should be relieved or not, but fear gave way to righteous anger. How dare some bastard mock Violet? Especially considering her writing was *good*. The teacher sounded like a frustrated, failed artist who needed to drag everyone down into failure with him.

Violet huffed out a soggy laugh. "Right? He's a super-dick."

Choosing her words as carefully as possible, Laurel said, "For what it's worth, I think you should talk to your dad. He'd tear that teacher to pieces."

"I know." The teen's world-weary sigh was worthy of someone three times her age. "But he's had a crazy year, and I didn't want to be a bigger pain for him, you know? It was already a lot that he had me in his house all the time."

"You know he loves you, Violet." Laurel cupped her jaw. "He would crawl over broken glass for you. It's been a tough year for both of you, and he still would have wanted to know if a teacher was being a bully."

"I know." Vi quickly swiped at her cheeks and smoothed her hair. "Ruth is coming up the road. We're supposed to babysit the twins for a couple of hours so Helen and Pedro can work."

"Maybe you should cancel, just this once."

Biting her lip, she shook her head. "No. I want to hang out with my friend." Her voice cracked. "Before I have to go back to not having any."

"Honey." Laurel took the girl's hands and squeezed. "Promise me you'll think about telling your dad how unhappy you are in LA. It would matter to him a lot."

"I promise."

She gave her best do-not-bullshit-me look. "Really, really?"

Vi's chuckle was watery. "Yes, really, really."

Then she stood and jogged over to meet Ruth. The two turned to wave goodbye to Laurel and cut across the grass toward the Cho-Diaz family's cabin. Once the girls vanished, Laurel waited for about five more minutes and then went in search of Neil. She wasn't going to break her promise to his daughter, but if they'd had a blow-up over the rock collection, he was going to be upset. He'd hide it better than Violet, but that didn't mean he'd feel any less pain.

"Hey." She pushed the screen door aside and walked in. "I just spoke to Vi. You okay?"

"I'm not sure." He rubbed his forehead and recounted his side of what had happened. Then he swallowed and confessed, "What if she has a problem with us being together? I haven't introduced her to any of my lady friends since the divorce. She knew they existed, but that's not the same. Or is this about Cara dying, some new stage of the grieving process? Or...maybe it's about Violet coming out as pansexual? God, I don't know."

Wow, he was way off. She had to choose her words carefully, so she kept her word to Vi, but didn't leave Neil in the dark. It sucked to be in the middle of a rock-hard place situation.

"You said she's gotten worse the closer she gets to the end of summer."

He rose and began to pace. "Yeah, but Vi's not going to freak this badly for this long just because she'll miss everyone."

"True enough." She pressed her lips together. "But when you leave here, you go back to LA."

"So?" He hunched his shoulders.

Yep, there was no way to clue him in without violating his daughter's trust, and she just couldn't do that. She tried a more direct approach. All she could do was get them to talk, but she wasn't telling tales. "It's not just a teen girl thing, Neil. It's not going to work itself out."

"Why?" He spun to face her. "What do you know that you haven't told me?"

"I can't tell you—I made a promise and I don't break those. But you really need to talk to Vi about what's bothering her." Laurel could only hope Vi forgave her for even saying this much. "Don't let her weasel out of telling you—it's important."

"Okay." His eyebrows rose and he crossed his arms, irritation radiating from him. "That's not ominous and vaguely terrifying."

Laurel matched his pose, notching her chin up. "She considers me a friend and confidante. Do you want her to have the kind of friend that will break promises?"

"I do if she's in danger," he snapped back. "Tell me what you know, Laurel. You have no right to keep important information about my daughter from me."

"I can't, Neil." She couldn't back down on this one. Jesus, their first real fight and it was over his child. What a nightmare. Cold fear quivered in her stomach. "Don't put me in that kind of position. I didn't have to say anything to you at all."

His nostrils flared, and she wasn't sure what he'd do. It was clear she'd scared him, and fighting with Violet had to have worried him too. They usually had such a good relationship. Would he take his fear out on Laurel, blame her for being the messenger of a more serious problem than teen angst?

"You're right." A vein throbbed in his temple, and his tone was little more than grudging. "Thanks for the head's up. I was planning to have a discussion with her when she got back anyway. I'm glad to know I need to push."

Laurel wrapped her arms around herself, still not reassured. "I made her promise to consider telling you, but that's the best I could do."

He considered her for a long moment before he walked over, pulled her into his embrace, and brushed a kiss over her forehead. "It's not your fault, sweetheart. I'm not mad at you. I'm just frustrated that Vi's keeping things from me. She's never done that before. I'm also not used to her confiding in someone besides me. Or Cara."

"I'm sorry." She leaned against him, wishing for all the world that she could make everything better for him. And for Violet. But there was nothing more Laurel could do. It was up to them to work it out. She knew they would. They did have a strong relationship, and they cared enough about each other to do whatever it took to make the other happy. Neil by coming to The Enclave when he hadn't planned to, Violet by not burdening him with being bullied by her teacher. Sure, Vi was a bit misguided, but she was a teenager. Even the mature ones had a lot to learn.

Still, Laurel hated being so powerless to really help. She guessed that was what being a parent must be like sometimes. It was every bit as scary and overwhelming as it sounded.

"Thank you for being here, for coming to talk to me." He sifted his fingers through her hair. "I know you didn't have to."

She huffed. "If you thought I was the kind of person who'd blithely let your kid do something self-destructive, you'd never have let me near her."

His chuckle was a rough sound under her ear. "True enough, sweetheart. True enough."

Whereas her own father had no problem letting young Laurel run with scissors as long as she didn't disturb his work or his schmoozing with clients.

Neil was waiting for his daughter when she got back from babysitting. What Laurel had said had worried him. He'd been working it over in his mind for the hour she'd been gone. Whatever was the matter with Vi, he needed to know. No matter how serious it was, they'd get through it together. That was what families did.

"Hey."

She straightened, her gaze reflecting instant wariness. That hurt, because Vi and he had never had that kind of knee-jerk negative re-action to each other. Worse, she looked scared. "Hey, Dad."

He waved to the other end of the couch. "Have a seat."

She didn't move from her spot by the door. "How long am I grounded for?"

"You're not." Because it wasn't retribution for her poor behavior and bad attitude he wanted. He needed information.

Surprise took some of the stiffness out of her shoulders. "I'm not?"

"Nope, but I do think we need to talk." He shifted so he sat facing her, one knee propped on the sofa.

"Talk? About what?"

He arched an eyebrow and didn't bother dignifying the question with a verbal response.

Her lips compressed, her fingers bunching into fists at her sides. "I'll get rid of some of the rocks."

"It's not about the rocks, is it?" Trying to maintain a relaxed pose took effort, because he didn't want her to think he was angry. Nothing would make her clam up faster. "So, why don't you tell me why the closer we get to going back to LA, the nastier you become? Is there something I need to know?"

"Laurel told you," she said dully, her entire body seeming to slump.

His gut clenched. "No, she didn't. I talked to her after you flounced out of here—not the first time in the last few weeks—and told her I was worried. I wasn't sure if this was just a growing pain I should let slide, if it was about you being pan, if it was about your mom, if it was about me and Laurel, if it was something else entirely. All she said was that she suspected it wasn't a growing pain. I asked why she'd think that and she refused to tell me anything else. She said I'd have to speak to you." He patted the seat cushion beside him. "So. Why don't you come tell me why you don't want to go home?"

"It's not my home!" The words exploded out of her with a ragged sob, as if a building volcano had finally erupted. "You don't even understand!"

"I'd like to." He kept his tone encouraging, leaning forward so she knew he listened.

The story came out in fits and starts, and he let her tell it without interruption. She paced back and forth in front of him and then flopped onto the couch, tears rolling down her cheeks. He snagged a box of tissues from the side table and handed it over. By the end, she was curled up against his side, blubbering all over his shirt while he held her tight and rocked her. A hundred emotions ricocheted through him as she spoke, rage at her asshole English teacher, self-loathing that he'd missed the signs that pointed to a major problem, pain for everything his baby girl had suffered this year. Especially when some of it was to protect him from worrying or being more stressed.

Laurel had been right. Saying yes to every opportunity meant he'd failed his daughter. He should have scaled back the moment she came to live with him, instead of trying to juggle everything. He'd dropped the most important ball, and he hadn't even noticed. It was his job to protect her, not the other way around.

The yes-game stopped now. As soon as he was back to the land of connectivity, he'd be having some serious discussions with his agent.

He'd hire an assistant if he had to.

Once Vi subsided to the occasion sniffle, he said, "We don't have to go back to LA, you know."

She leaned away from him, her gaze searching his face, hope and disbelief warring in her expression. "We...we don't?"

"We can live anywhere in the US we want. Anywhere in the world, really." Then he held up a hand. "Okay, anywhere that has decent internet and cell reception, so this area is out."

"You're serious?" She all but quivered in excitement. "We don't have to go back. Oh my God. I can't even—"

She launched herself at him, wrapping her arms around his neck in a stranglehold. He choked a little, and she backed off with a laugh, though tears glistened in her eyes.

"Do you want to move back to Maine? You know I didn't sell the house." It was the house that Cara and he had bought when they'd gotten their first major book advances. It was the house Cara had continued to raise their daughter in after the divorce. He had no intention of selling the place. It was Violet's inheritance—she could decide what to do with the property when she was old enough.

He'd asked her if she wanted to keep living there after her mother died, and she'd said no. Maybe she'd changed her mind. If she'd rather live in Maine, he'd uproot his life in California and move back to his home state. She'd spent a year being bullied by an adult who should have looked out for her best interest, helped her to grow her writing talents. At the moment, Neil would have lived on the moon if it was what she wanted.

She pressed her lips together and slowly shook her head, appearing uncertain. "I think...there'd still be too many memories of Mom. Maybe I could go back someday, but not yet."

"But you don't want to live in LA," he prompted.

"No!" That was definitive, at least. Her hair flew out wildly as she shook her head.

"Okay." He smoothed her curls back. "What place sounds good to you, baby girl?"

She was quiet for a long time. "I want us to live wherever Laurel lives."

That hit him like a kick in the gut. Living with Laurel...God, yes. Tangling her up in the madness of his life...hell no. "I think she moves around a lot, Vi. That wouldn't work with your schooling."

"She might stay put if, like, she knew we wanted her to. We could ask her to move in with us." Her tone was so matter-of-fact, as if she couldn't believe he hadn't figured this out for himself already.

"Violet." He shook his head.

"Think about it." She tugged on his shirt sleeve. "It'd be awesome."

It would be.

"You love her. I love her. It's simple. Why do grown-ups have to make everything all complicated?" She arched her brows. "She's never going to replace Mom, but she's awesome step-mom material. If you know what I mean."

Yeah, because that hint was so subtle.

"I'll think about it," he said, and he would think about it, but he already knew his answer would be no. Even though he wanted it to be yes.

"Can I take all my rocks with me?" She widened her eyes appealingly. "We can just ship them instead of lugging them along in the suitcases. And this way they're already packed for the move. It's perfect!"

"All right." He gave in gracefully. "You can keep the rocks."

A wide smile flashed across her face. "Thanks for letting me win that one."

"You're welcome." He ruffled her hair, and she squawked, leaping to her feet.

"Can I get my hair streaked like Lau—"

"No, and you can't have a pony either." He rolled his eyes. "Don't push your luck, kid."

"It was worth a try," she countered, totally unrepentant.

"We should probably get ready for bed. Do you want to shower first?" He pushed to his feet, but staggered when she plowed into him, giving him another hug before she pulled away to dance toward her bedroom.

"No more LA, no more stupid kids, no more jerkwad teachers." She twirled in a circle. "Yeeeeeeeeeeesssssss!"

"I'll assume that means you want the bathroom first," he replied drily, though her enthusiasm stabbed at his soul as he resumed his seat. How had he not seen that her misery the past year wasn't all about losing Cara? Why had he never pressed when she hadn't talked about her school much? He'd known she hadn't made many close friends but hadn't realized she'd felt quite so ostracized.

He felt like the worst parent on the planet. Self-disgust curdled in his belly, and he dropped his head back against the couch, closing his eyes. He'd never wanted to crawl into a hole more in his entire life. At least when he'd lost his unborn son, there was nothing he could have done. This, he should have prevented. He could have, if he weren't an overextended, cluelessly pathetic excuse for a father.

"Hey, Dad?"

He straightened to look at her. "Yes, baby?"

She propped one foot on top of the other, her pajamas clutched in a bundle under her arm. "I really would like to keep Laurel."

"I know." His voice sounded like gravel in a blender. God, he'd love to have Laurel near now, but she didn't deserve to constantly be burdened with his problems. She'd helped him shoulder the load this summer, but no one wanted to clean up someone else's mess forever. Which was what would happen to her if he tried to convince her to stick around.

"I think she'd like to keep us too." Vi gave him an encouraging smile.

He nodded but made no other reply.

She looked like she was going to say more, but just walked over and kissed his cheek before going to shower. Which left him alone with his thoughts. A dangerous thing in the frame of mind he was in, surfing down an ugly shame spiral.

If anything, he was even less willing to try to drag Laurel deeper into his quagmire. He'd been cocksure going into his first marriage—his last real relationship—and look how well that had turned out. He was older and hopefully a little wiser now, and he could see how badly he could screw up a second try. He'd screwed up the first time, he was screwing up single parenthood, he was only barely managing to finish his writing projects—hell, he was just a gigantic screw up right now.

Saddling Laurel with someone like him would be a crime.

It didn't matter how desperately he loved her; he needed to end this thing they had, for her own good.

He was sure she'd keep in touch with Vi when summer ended, and while the father in him was grateful, the man in him knew it was going to burn like hellfire to see her and hear about her and not have her in his arms.

Ever again.

CHAPTER TEN

Neil had been strangely quiet for most of the week, burying himself in work, and it was becoming seriously worrisome. The day after tomorrow was the last day in Colorado. Less than forty-eight hours left. Laurel saw him at meals and during kitchen duty like usual, but that was it. She hadn't spent the night—or even gotten in a quickie—since he'd quarreled with Violet. He seemed to be brooding. She didn't have to think very hard to know what he was dwelling on. She'd tried to give him breathing room, but the time they had left was ticking down to nothing. Maybe it was time to talk.

But she'd hesitated to do so because it also seemed like he might be avoiding her. He'd gone into Denver for a few days to meet with the TV station rep about the possible show, and he hadn't invited her. In fact, she hadn't even known he'd gone until Mimi mentioned something casually. Hadn't that been embarrassing? Because it had been painfully obvious to the other woman after about three sentences that Laurel knew nothing about the trip.

She stepped out of her cabin into afternoon sunshine and hurried toward the lodge for lunch. She needed caffeine something fierce today. It had been difficult to sleep lately, both because she'd gotten so used to Neil holding her in the night, and because she was plagued by questions that wouldn't stop.

Was the avoidance a sign that he was upset Violet had talked to her and not him about being bullied? Was he trying to put distance between her and his daughter? As far as she knew, he hadn't limited Vi's contact with Laurel, just his own.

Which meant she was mostly just baffled and hurt.

And deep down, she wondered if this meant he'd decided to end their affair, but hadn't found a non-awkward way to tell her it was over. So he was just keeping himself occupied until the summer was over and he could walk away. She really didn't want that to be the case, but she had to acknowledge the possibility.

She entered the lodge and followed the crowd to the buffet. Loading up on coffee, soup, fruit, and a sandwich, she turned to scan the room for an empty table. She wasn't really interested in company.

"Laurel!" Violet waved from a spot near the window, her curls bouncing with the vigor of her movements.

Crap. For the first time, she didn't want to sit with them. She didn't think she could endure Neil's silent treatment, but there seemed no graceful way out of it. Hurting Vi's feelings wasn't an option.

Vi dominated the conversation during the meal, with Laurel and Neil only needing to respond to direct questions. When his daughter got up for another serving of sliced cantaloupe, Laurel took a breath and tried for some small talk.

"I heard you finished your screenplay." And it had stung to have to hear that from Vi instead of Neil, but Laurel kept that small pain to herself.

"A draft of it, yes." He flicked a glance at her but refocused on his lunch too fast for her to read his expression. "I'm nowhere near done."

Arching a brow, she asked, "Didn't you promise to have a draft done by the end of the program?"

He hunched a shoulder. "Yes."

The lack of eye contact became unsettling. "So you fulfilled your obligations for the summer. Congrats."

His snort was derisive, his tone condescending. "The work never stops."

It took serious effort not to snap, and her teeth ground together. "No one's work ever stops, Neil, but it's okay to take a break and celebrate when you reach an important goal. Which you've done, and under tremendous pressure."

"Yeah."

That was all. But it was enough to make her frustration boiled over.

"What's this about, Neil? Is it Violet getting bullied?"

He flinched a bit. "It's nothing, Laurel."

"You're beating yourself up, aren't you?" She leaned toward him. "You're not a failure as a father, Neil. Don't think that."

He cut a blistering glance at her but said nothing.

She sighed. "She takes too much on herself...a lot like her dad."

"I don't want to discuss this." He stabbed at a piece of melon on his plate, his brows drawn together in a scowl.

"She's growing up, Neil. She's going to stumble and make mistakes. She's going to want to be more independent, to try to handle things on her own. That's part of becoming an adult. When she needs you, she'll come to you."

His gray gaze was darker than a stormy sea. "She came to you first."

"She considers me a friend." She threw up her hands. "Friends are who you tell secrets to. Dads are who you go to when you need rescuing."

"She never used to keep things from me before. Especially nothing that important."

"It's really that shocking?" She sniffed in disdain. "Isn't this around the age you started keeping things from your parents too? Sneaking out late with the guys, kissing girls—"

He didn't refute her, just doggedly stuck to his guns. "I should have been paying better attention. The bottom line is, I screwed up. I should have asked more questions about her school."

"But her grades didn't slip, right?" She pressed her point. "And she didn't complain about anything, so of course your focus was on this huge loss she'd suffered. Why would you assume otherwise?"

"Leave it alone, Laurel. I don't want to talk about it." His voice cracked like a whip.

She leaned back, a quiver of unease and fear passing through her. Swallowing, she said carefully, "You don't want to talk about it at all, or you just don't want to talk to *me* about it?"

"Does it matter?" His tone went cool.

She nodded slowly. "Yes, I think the distinction is an important one."

"You can take it however you want. I have work to do. I'm too busy to quibble with you over semantics." With that, he rose and walked away, ripping her heart out in the process.

She pressed a hand to her chest, stunned by the blow she hadn't seen coming. His words were so like something her father would say to her that she felt small and stupid, just as she had her entire childhood. As if she wasn't good enough, as if she wasn't worth his time, and no matter what she did to get attention, it was never going to be enough. With her parents, she'd learned to accept that she just wasn't the type of daughter they wanted—too artsy, not serious enough, too different from the people they associated with. That wasn't her fault.

Neil knew that, and he was still treating her the same way. It was a betrayal that was almost crippling in the agony it caused her. It was her worst fears wrapped up in one terrifying package. She loved him. Desperately. He was every bit the workaholic her father was, and she was his last priority. Worse, she simply wasn't a priority. Remembering his cold, distant expression, it was difficult to convince herself he even cared at all.

Dropping her gaze to her plate, she refused to watch him walk away. There was no way to force someone to give a damn about you, to love you. He couldn't have made it any clearer that he was done with her, with them, with whatever they'd had together this summer. That maybe there was never a *them* to begin with.

He was just one more man she loved who'd decided she was an unnecessary, bothersome mistake he wanted to put behind him. Bile coated her tongue and she wanted to vomit.

Violet walked up, concern on her face. She glanced from Neil's retreating back to Laurel. "Are you and Dad fighting?"

Agony and impending loss squeezed her insides. "No, we're not."

They weren't fighting, they weren't fucking, they weren't talking, they weren't...anything. But that wasn't something she cared to discuss with Violet.

The girl parked herself next to Laurel. "Ruth and me are meeting up to play pool after lunch. We're also going to set up her Instagram account and follow each other. Since she turned thirteen this summer, her parents say she can join."

"When does Ruth go back to Seattle?" Tucking a lock of hair behind her ear, Laurel dragged herself from her misery to focus on the girl she adored.

"Her parents are coming to get her a few days after everyone leaves. Too bad I don't get to meet them." Vi waggled her eyebrows. "I bet they're as cray-cray as Gloria."

"No one's as cray-cray as Gloria."

She giggled. "True story."

Laurel gave the teen a one-armed hug. She was going to miss her so much, despite how her dad had just ditched Laurel. "How's your book going?"

"Pretty good." Violet leaned into the embrace. "I didn't finish the first draft like I planned, but I didn't think there'd be anyone here to hang out with. Or babysit."

"The best things in life are often the ones we don't expect."

Vi nodded. "Like you and Dad getting together."

Oh God. Laurel snatched up her cold coffee and took a deep swig. She would not cry, she would *not* cry. Not in public and not in front of Vi. She'd save that for when she got back to her cabin. "You know we might not stay together when we leave. Not every good thing in life is for keeps. But you and I can stay friends, even if your dad and I don't. We can email or Facebook or whatever social network you prefer. I get down to LA for gallery showings a few times a year. I'm sure your dad wouldn't mind us doing lunch or shopping or hanging out at the beach."

"We won't be in LA though. We're moving." Expectation shone in Vi's gaze, as if Laurel should know something that she didn't.

But shock was rippling through her. One more thing to prove Neil was over her and moving on, literally and figuratively. When her voice emerged, it sounded almost normal. "Oh, yeah? Talked to your dad about hating it there, huh?"

"Thanks to you. I'm glad you didn't tell him everything."

"I promised you I wouldn't. I'd never break a promise to you...unless I really thought you were a danger to yourself or others." She gave the teen a look. "We were pretty close this time."

Heaving a deep sigh, Violet wrinkled her nose. "Yeah."

"So, where to, if not LA?" Laurel dropped a kiss on the girl's crown and then tidied her tray. She really needed some alone time to bawl her eyes out. "I have a suitcase and a passport. I can travel anywhere if we need a visit."

"I don't know yet. Dad and I are talking. We'll need to go back to pack our stuff and house hunt in other places." Something calculating flashed in Vi's gaze. "Where would you go if you could live anywhere?"

Wasn't that a thought Laurel had had more than once lately? "I'm thinking about buying a place close to my brother in Half Moon Bay. Maybe be there more for my nephew growing up."

Where else did she have to go? She'd hoped, way down deep where she didn't have to admit it to anyone, that she might be spending more time with Neil after the program ended. That maybe she might find the place she belonged—not a location but a person. The right person—the right sort of man. The one who, no matter where they were on Earth, as long as she was with him, she was home.

But she'd been wrong.

N eil felt like shit. Complete, utter, unmitigated shit. He'd watched the hurt and confusion reflect in Laurel's gaze, saw when he'd landed a killing emotional blow, and hated himself when he'd left her sitting alone. For the millionth time, he ran through the reasons why it was the best thing for her, why she deserved better, but it didn't help. He still just felt like shit. She was determined enough that if he hadn't pushed her away, and pushed hard, that she might have tried to talk him into continuing their relationship.

And he didn't have the willpower to say no. So he'd acted like an asshole.

He worked the rest of the afternoon on his script, had dinner with Vi and Ruth—who decided to continue teaching themselves to play pool—then went back to the cabin and did some packing, then read through Helen's new pages. She was progressing well and had added several particularly gruesome plot twists. It was great stuff, and he had to admit it was one of the few things he felt good about these days.

In the distance, he heard a screen door slam, and he glanced out the open window to see Laurel leaving her cabin. It took every ounce of self-control not to call out to her. He wanted her near, missed her so much it was a physical ache inside him.

How the hell was he going to make it through the rest of the trip without her? For that matter, what about the rest of his life? It utterly sucked to take the high road sometimes, to put the person you loved above yourself and your needs.

The sound of footsteps on gravel made his heart leap, and he was on his feet before his brain could catch up. "Lau—oh, hey, Helen."

"Hey, boss." His protégé stood at the bottom of the steps, the fading sunlight playing off her jet-black hair. "I came to see if the revisions I did were working for you."

Well, this was a first. She usually scheduled meetings with him so she could coordinate toddler duty with her husband or babysitters. He held open the screen door. "Yeah, they're great. I think this should be the final round and then you're ready to start thinking seriously about publishing."

"Awesome." She didn't come in. "Care to join me for a walk? I'm supposed to be home soon. It's best not to leave Pedro outnumbered for long. He can be a little too laid back about what the kids get into, you know?"

Curiouser and curiouser. "Sure, let me grab a sweatshirt. It's going to get chilly tonight."

"It's the elevation. It'd still be roasting and muggy in Texas all night long."

"Yeah." As he shrugged into his hoodie, he tried not to recall the day he'd forgotten it and Laurel had returned it. The first time they'd made love. It felt like just yesterday, but he also felt like a different man from the one who'd arrived here.

He stepped out and they set off down the road. Helen was remarkably quiet, but he could feel her gaze on him as she kept glancing his way. Clearly, she wanted to talk about something, but he decided to wait her out rather than asking. His mentee wasn't the type to remain silent long. Quite the opposite, actually.

Finally, she heaved a small sigh. "You want to talk about it?"

"About what?" With her, the options were pretty limitless.

Her face scrunched. "There are few enough of us here that if you have a little tiff over lunch, people are going to notice."

"And gossip, apparently." Christ. The last thing he wanted people speculating about was Laurel and him. They'd been a popular topic when they'd first begun dating, but this was different.

"Gossip goes without saying." Helen flicked her fingers. "But I was worried about you when I heard, so I came over."

He shoved his fists into the front pocket of his hoodie. "I thought you came to discuss your pages."

"I'm a woman. I multitask." She shrugged as if this was obvious.

"Of course." But he didn't want to talk about how things were going with Laurel, or his sense of failure as a parent and a person. Nope, those things were not on the table for discussion. So, maybe it was time to sidetrack his protégé in a big way. He'd gotten some important news for her that morning but had wanted to wait to tell her in person. Her reaction was going to be too good to miss. "So...I'm recommending you to my agent."

Her breath caught audibly, and for the first time in three months, she seemed utterly speechless.

"Actually, no," he mused. "That's not true."

That breath whooshed out, but still no words were forthcoming.

"I already recommended you to him. And sent your first three chapters to him. I thought we'd polished them to a point that they were more than ready." He watched her from the corner of his eye, thoroughly amused for the first time in days. When he thought she might be ready to explode from the waiting, he casually mentioned, "My agent would like to see the full manuscript, but thinks it's at a point where he can start shopping the proposal to publishers. He'd like to speak to you over the phone when you have a free moment. He hoped tomorrow, one o'clock eastern time. Would you like his number?"

"Would I—" She all but picked him up, she hugged him so hard. "Oh, shit! This is awesome. Neil, you're the most amazing mentor of all time! You know you have the best agent in the business, right? You know he was on my never-going-to-happen list, right?"

He patted her shoulder, grinning at her fervor. "I know, but I think you'll suit each other, and he's got the contacts and clout to get you a kick-ass first contract. I think there's a market for your work, and so does my agent, which is more important."

"If I couldn't sell it to a big publisher, I was going to self-publish it and hope for the best, but I really did want the traditional publishing route. That was always my dream, to see my books in stores, not just print-on-demand and ebook."

"You're babbling, Helen."

"I know." She hung on his arm as if she feared she'd fall. "It's either that or cry."

"No crying. Please." He urged her down the road, grateful when he saw the mammoth bulk of the lodge come into view.

"I won't. I won't. I promise." She sniffled several times as they walked but managed to keep it together. "Oh, there's Laurel and Mimi. I have to tell them."

She dragged him along with her, though he didn't exactly resist. It was a masochistic pleasure to see Laurel. She sat on the porch with Mimi. They'd propped their feet on the railing and each held a goblet of red wine. The two women went dead silent as Helen and Neil approached, which gave him a hint of what they might have been discussing. He doubted it had been flattering to him, and he felt heat flood his cheeks.

He nodded, keeping his voice even. "Mimi. Laurel."

"Graves." Laurel's expression was as blank and smooth as glass, not a single emotion showing.

Mimi just nodded back, the most hostile look he'd ever seen morphing her normally friendly face. Yep, tales of his assholery had been told. He deserved nothing less, did he? He'd known what he was doing, and his plan had been effective. He was a piece of shit, and everyone knew it. Helen offered him a pitying glance, which he wasn't sure was better than the hostility.

"Did you need something?" Laurel asked coolly.

Neil shrugged. "Helen had some news she wanted to share."

That seemed to jog his protégé into speech. She blurted out her news and the three women squealed and hugged and babbled a rush of words he didn't quite catch. They wouldn't have welcomed his participation in the revelry, so he stood apart and watched the joyful merriment. Ostracism—something else he deserved.

His daughter chose that moment to pop out of the lodge, her eyes going wide as she took in the tangled three-way hug. "Hey, guys. You're being loud. What's going on?"

"Your dad hooked me up with his agent." Helen sounded a bit breathy and quickly dabbed at her eyes. "But I'm not going to cry. Yet."

Time for a topic change, because he was pretty sure Mimi had started tearing up and if one woman went, it'd turn into a gigantic sobfest. "How was the pool game with Ruth, honey?"

"We both suck at it." Vi stuck her hands in her jean pockets. "But we had a good time."

"That's good." He held out his hand, and she came to loop her arm around his waist.

"I need to go tell my husband. And rescue him from the children." Helen's smile was radiant. "Oh, Vi, if you could babysit for me around eleven tomorrow while I talk to my new maybe-agent, I would kiss you all over your head."

"Or you could just pay me my usual rate." Vi's nose wrinkled. "With no kissing or crying."

"Gee, who does that remind me of?" Helen drawled.

"It's, like, genetic. I can't be blamed for DNA." Violet grinned guilelessly, then turned to Laurel. "Walk back with us? It's getting dark."

She pushed back a lock of teal-streaked hair. "And someone might try to mug me?"

"A bear could eat you," his daughter insisted. "Or a serial killer."

"A serial killer could eat me?" Amusement lilted Laurel's tone. "Man, you've been reading too many of your dad's books. It's warped you."

She dimpled.

"I like it," Helen mused. "I might have to put that in a novel."

Vi arched her eyebrows. "Dedicate it to me?"

"It's a deal." Helen jogged down the porch steps. "Okay, I'm off.

See you in the morning, when I will still be floating on cloud nine."

"Good night!" Mimi picked up the discarded wine glasses and cast Neil one last glare before she went inside.

Helen headed down one road while Neil, Violet, and Laurel followed another in the direction of their respective cabins. Vi walked on Neil's left and seemed to be bumping into him to nudge him toward Laurel on his right. She tensed as his arm brushed hers, and he bled inside when she sidestepped to avoid him.

Yeah, he really had screwed everything up, hadn't he? But that had been his intention when he'd decided to end things. Everything in his life was up in the air—he was moving to God-knew-where and trying to overhaul his career path, but it was going to be at least another year before he dug out from all his current contracts. Even with a new as-yet-unhired assistant, he was going to be strapped for time for a good long while yet. She would hate that. It would remind her too much of her upbringing.

A clean cut was better for her.

They reached her place, and as much as he was tempted to linger, to have just a few more minutes in her presence, he made himself keep walking.

"Hey, Vi. Can you give us a sec?"

He froze in place, while his daughter blithely continued along. "Good night, Laurel! See you at breakfast!"

It took every ounce of courage he could muster to turn and face her. "You wanted to say something?"

The porch light shone stark on her countenance, casting her lovely face into shadows and light. Her mouth opened, then closed. He could see pain and anger in her gaze. Her mouth tightened and she shook her head. "So, that's it? Wham, bam, thank you, ma'am, and now we're done? I wasn't even worth a mature breakup?" Tears shone in her eyes.

"You didn't care about me at all, did you?"

A lie that big couldn't cross his lips, even though that would put a final nail in the coffin. So he did the one thing he could do—hauled her into his arms to claim a last, soul-searing kiss. Maybe he could burn the taste of her into his memory forever, so he'd never forget it.

One final taste. That was all he could allow himself.

She kissed him back, but her fist slammed against his shoulder, as much anger as passion in the contact. It was all lips and teeth and tongues. His hands were everywhere, molding her curves. His shaft went rigid in seconds, a response that was as instinctive as breathing when she was near. Her fingers twined through his hair, her grip almost painful, sending prickles down his scalp. She changed the angle of the kiss, nipping at his lower lip. He couldn't hold back a groan and cupped her backside to fit her tighter to him.

No. He needed to stop or he wouldn't be able to. He'd drag her into her cabin and do something they'd both regret. He broke his mouth away from hers.

"I'm sorry, Laurel." And then he ripped himself out of her embrace and made himself walk away.

He'd never hated himself more.

CHAPTER ELEVEN

This was it. The very last night. Her bags were packed, her canvases were crated up to be shipped. All but one. This one was a gift for Neil and Vi. And maybe just Vi if Neil continued to give her that blank stare he'd been aiming her way all week. He'd only managed a polite nod during the end-of-summer barbeque Mimi and Gloria had hosted for everyone. Ruth and Violet had kept the chatter going whenever they'd been together, thankfully, because Laurel couldn't even look at him anymore. Especially not after that last kiss. She just wanted to crawl in a hole and die when he was nearby. It hadn't helped that every single soul at The Enclave noticed the sudden distance between them.

She'd said goodbye to all the people she'd gotten close to, shook hands with her still-reclusive mentee, who'd thanked her profusely—for him—for all her help. That felt good. A lot of what was accomplished this summer felt good.

Except for one thing. One huge, massive, heart-wrenching thing.

Neil Graves.

She'd tried to talk herself down since their last kiss. They'd never intended for the affair to last after the program ended. No promises were ever made. She had no right to feel cheated, hurt, or let down.

Bullshit.

That was exactly the kind of mentality she'd operated under her entire life—she wasn't good enough to deserve more, she should be willing to accept less than what she wanted from the people she loved.

It was time to get over that. Starting right now. Neil and she needed to have a talk, whether he liked it or not. She needed to tell him, flat out, how she felt, both good and bad. She doubted he'd care to hear it, but she wasn't going to walk away feeling this soul-deep pain like she did when she had to visit with her parents. It was tempting to slink away with her tail tucked between her legs, but she'd promised herself she'd be braver with her heart, that she'd reach for what she really wanted.

So, she needed to make that reach. She was probably going to fall on her face, but she intended to speak her piece, and even though she loved him, she also deserved to be treated better than he had the last week. She had more than earned a proper goodbye and at least a thank you for being an amazing friend to both Graveses over the summer. He owed her that much.

"You can do this, Laurel. You can do this."

Yeah, she was talking to herself now. It helped gird her loins.

She hoisted the painting into her arms and exited her cabin. Dinner had been a couple of hours ago, and the sun was starting to set. The lights were on next door, so she knew they hadn't left to visit anyone. It felt like the longest walk of her life to travel the short distance between her place and theirs. Her knees actually trembled, and if she weren't holding the canvas, she was fairly sure her hands would be shaking.

Nerves pinged through her, and her stomach did summersaults. Her heart pounded so loudly, it drowned out the twilight sounds of the surrounding forest.

Part of her dreaded the coming confrontation and part of her wanted to kick Neil Graves's cute ass from here into the next state. No matter what, they were going to have this discussion. Even if she had to drag him out of his cabin by the ear to make him listen to what she had to say.

"Laurel!" Violet threw the door wide before Laurel reached it. "What do you have there?"

"A going-away present. May I come in?"

"Like you need to ask." Vi rolled her eyes and held open the door. Neil appeared behind his daughter, watching Laurel steadily, and not protesting when she stepped into the house. Vi danced around her. "Is that a painting? Is it for us? OMG! Dad, we have a Laurel Patton piece. Can it hang in my room in our new house?"

"Sure, it can hang in your room." Neil's grin was indulgent.

So he didn't have to look at it? Laurel shook that thought away and pulled the canvas out from under her arm. "You haven't even seen it yet. You might want to hang it in the attic if you don't like it."

"I love it," Vi said staunchly, before Laurel even turned the painting around for her to see. "All your work is amazing."

"I wish that were true." Laurel set the canvas on top of the desk, propping it against the wall and stepping back. "But I love you for saying so."

Vi laced her arms around Laurel's waist. "I love you too. I'm going to miss you so much."

"Me too, sweetie." She bent to hug the girl closer, emotions clogging her throat and making the backs of her eyes burn. "Me too. But I'll come visit soon."

"Promise?" Vi whispered in her ear.

Laurel nodded and held the teen tight, rocking her a little. "I promise."

They pulled back and both of them swiped at their eyes. Vi managed a little smile and gestured to the canvas. "Well, I'll get to look at your painting every day until then. It really is dope."

"I'm glad you like it." Laurel glanced quickly at Neil, whose expression was unreadable. "I'll crate it up and ship it to whatever address you'd like. I have the one in LA, but if you'd rather I—"

"The one in LA is fine," he interjected. "It'll take us some time to move, and we still need to shop for a new place."

"Okay then." She drew in a giant lungful of air, and his gaze flickered for just a moment to her breasts. Well, at least that hadn't changed. She met his gaze squarely. "I'd like a private word."

"I can go. Ruth asked me to spend the last night at her house anyway and I said I'd check." Vi glanced between her dad and Laurel. "So...is that okay?"

Since it wasn't clear who she was asking permission from, Laurel nodded while Neil said, "Sure. Have fun, baby."

"I'm not a baby," the teen huffed.

"I cleaned up your puke and changed your diaper, kiddo." He dipped a shoulder in a shrug. "You'll always be my baby, no matter how old you get. Deal with it."

"Diapers, really? That's nasty, Dad." She made a gagging motion.

"It really was. Like this one time—"

"And I'm out. I'll see you in the morning to say goodbye, Laurel." She hugged Laurel, kissed Neil on the cheek, grabbed a pre-packed overnight bag from her room, and bolted for the front door.

Well, they were alone, though this wasn't exactly what Laurel had had in mind. "You know how to clear a room, Graves."

"Blood, death, gross," he quipped.

A half-smile tilted up her lips. "I remember."

"You wanted to talk." He settled on the arm of the couch, crossing his arms over his broad chest. "I'm listening."

"You were an ass to me this week. You hurt me and you did it on purpose." Okay, not the classiest opening, but it got straight to the point. She lifted her chin, daring him to refute her.

"I know." His tone was undefensive. "You're right. I handled things badly. I'm sorry."

"Good, but being sorry isn't enough. I want you to tell me why."

He nodded slowly. "We agreed that things between us would end at the end of summer. What happened with Violet made me realize that that really was best, though I bungled everything with her and you. I did—I do—care about you, Laurel. You were amazing to both my daughter and me, and I don't think we'd have made it through without you. I know I'll never forget you."

The finality in his voice made her heart ache. He'd made his decision and that was it. But what else did she want? She'd gotten her thank you and goodbye. It was time to leave. He wasn't interested in more than what they'd already had, he'd been clear about that.

But she hadn't said everything she wanted, even if he'd said what she'd thought she wanted to hear. "Why is it best that we stop seeing each other? If you care about me and won't forget me...why let it end? Just because we planned it that way? That seems ridiculous."

"Please don't make this harder, sweetheart." For a split-second, utter torment filled his gaze, but then it was gone again, and the stoic mask was once again in place.

"You're the one making it hard." Moisture stung her eyes, blurring her vision. She blinked back the tears. "It's our last night. I want to be with you."

He straightened, rising to his feet. "It wouldn't change anything."

"Do you want me to leave or stay? It's that simple."

"Stay." The word shot out of him. "But—"

"Shut up and take your clothes off, Neil." She tugged her shirt over her head and tossed it at him. He caught it midair, and then he took in the fact that she wasn't wearing a bra. The lust that flared in his gaze was nice, but sex wasn't why she'd come over here. She looked him straight in the eye and made herself more vulnerable than she'd ever been in her life, knowing that she wasn't going to get through this night unscathed. "I love you, Neil. I know you don't feel the same. I know you're leaving in the morning, but I needed to say it and needed you to hear it."

"I hear you." His voice was ragged, the hand holding her shirt hanging limply by his side.

"Okay then." She flicked open the button on her jeans. "Let's get busy."

"Laurel, I—"

"Unless you're going to say you adore me and want to marry me and live happily ever after, then I really don't want to hear it." She stepped toward him. If this was it, she intended to make the most of every second. She was going to glut herself on the feel of him over her, inside her.

"I just—" He shook his head, cutting himself off.

When she was close enough to touch him, she set her palm on his chest and slid it down his stomach to grasp his shaft. He sucked in a breath as she stroked him through his pants. His erection grew thick and hard beneath her fingers, and when she looked up at his face, his eyes were pinched closed and he appeared as if he were in the throes of agony. He didn't try to stop her or rush her, even when shudders began to wrack his big body.

"Enjoying yourself, Graves?"

"Yes," he rasped. "Just letting you have your way with me."

She tugged on his shaft, making his eyes flare wide. "Let's take this into the other room. I'm going to need a comfortable mattress for what I have in mind."

After turning, she sauntered toward his bedroom. He followed so closely behind her that she could feel the heat of him against her bare back. Discarding her clothes along the way, she heard him do the same. Desire flowed through her, and each step made her thighs brush together, ratcheting up her need. She'd never wanted anyone the way she wanted him and had one night to get her fill.

She was naked by the time she reached the nightstand and flicked on the lamp. Glancing over her shoulder, she saw he was both nude and flagrantly aroused. His erection danced in a hard arc below his navel. Very nice. She bit her lip and debated whether she wanted to start with a blowjob or get right to the main event.

His dark eyebrows rose. "Are you just going to stare?"

"Nope." Without a word of warning, she planted her hands on his chest and shoved him back on the bed.

The surprised sound he made was cut off as he bounced against the mattress. He folded his arms behind his head. "What will you do with me?"

"Whatever I want." She slipped onto the bed and knelt beside him. Curling her fingers around his erection, she gave him a siren's smile.

Bending forward, she swirled her tongue around the bulbous crest, and he shuddered beneath her. His scent was warm and musky and erotic, and she grew even wetter, knowing how much he wanted her. Sucking him into her mouth, she took the length of him in until he nudged the back of her throat. He groaned and swore as she eased his shaft from her mouth, then sank down again. Fast, then slow. Toying with him, making the speed too irregular to let him come. But it was more than enough to have him quivering with need.

His hand slid into her hair, trying to push her faster, but she resisted, humming a protest. As she'd intended, the vibrations along his shaft left him gasping. She liked the power of having him at her mercy. Considering she felt so helpless to stop him from ending their relationship, she'd take this opportunity to relish a little sensual revenge. She let her teeth scrape lightly against the underside of his shaft and felt him pulse in her mouth.

"Christ, sweetheart. I'm dying here."

Lucky for him, she was done teasing. She needed him now. He panted when she let him slip from between her lips. She twisted around and reached for the condoms in his nightstand. After pulling a rubber out, she ripped it open and slipped it onto his erection. She spread her fingers over his chest, making sure to brush over his small nipples.

His breath hissed in, and his fists balled in the sheets. "Please, Laurel."

"Begging. Nice." She gave him a cheeky grin. "But I want you on top of me."

"Yes," he groaned.

He hooked an arm around her waist, pulled her down beside him, and rolled atop her. His weight pressed her thighs to the mattress, and she felt the hot probing of his shaft before he slid deep inside her. Yes, that was exactly how she wanted it. She linked her fingers behind his neck, holding him close.

"Make it good for me, Graves." Because it was their last time. She didn't voice the last part, but she could see on his face that he understood what she'd meant.

He arched one supercilious eyebrow. "Have I ever let you down in bed, Patton?"

She cinched her legs around his hips. "Don't make this a first."

"Never," he vowed. And then he went about proving it.

After shifting to the left, he slipped a hand between them to fondle her breast. Her nipples contracted to stiff points, and the side he wasn't touching was pressed to the curls on his chest—every time either of them took a breath, there was a slight rasp that turned her on even more. When his fingers zeroed in on her other nipple, pinching and rolling the taut crest, she bit her lip.

"Ah, ah, ah. That's my job." He released her breast to dip forward and catch her lip between his teeth. He slipped his tongue into her mouth, and she squirmed as white-hot lust simmered within her. She was so slick, so greedy for him.

While he kissed her, he began rotating his pelvis to grind against her nub. Each pass was a leisurely stimulation of that tight bundle of nerves. She pressed her hips higher to take him deeper, wanting more, wanting it now. He obliged her silent demand, withdrawing and plunging into her. She broke her lips from his, gasping for air. Her heart hammered in her ears, and her breathing rasped. "Neil!"

Climax built within her with each forceful thrust, and shivers ran through her when he filled her. Their movements were in perfect sync, their eyes locking as they raced to the edge of sanity. A smile flashed across his face, so sinful it made her toes curl. He reached down and hitched her leg higher around his waist, driving in at a steeper angle that let him hit just the right spot inside her. Goose bumps broke across her skin. God, that felt so damn good, her eyes almost rolled back in her head. But she couldn't look away from him, needing to see and experience every single second.

He threw his head back, his neck cording as he struggled for control. It hit her that she'd never see him like this again, all civility stripped away until only the raw, wild man remained. It was a side of himself he rarely unleashed, except here with her. She'd miss that. One of a million little things she'd miss about him.

"I love you," she whispered, her heart breaking as she arched under him. Her palms glided down his spine, and she sank her nails into his flexing buttocks, urging him to move faster, to send them both flying into oblivion.

He gave her exactly what she wanted, increasing his speed so he powered into her. Then he dipped forward and bit down on the sensitive tendon that connected shoulder to neck.

It was more than enough.

Pinpricks of light exploded behind her lids and she tumbled headlong into orgasm. He groaned and followed her, shuddering in her and over her. He collapsed on top of her, and she held him tight. But her high didn't last as long as normal, because reality kept coming back to haunt her. Pain stabbed at her soul, knowing no matter how many times she'd see him after this, it would never be the same again. He'd never be hers again. She buried her face in his neck, not wanting him to notice the tears in her eyes. This was goodbye. Far too soon, she'd need to get up, put on her clothes, and leave.

She didn't know how she'd survive it.

"I love you, Neil. I love you so much."

N eil opened his eyes and stared into the pre-dawn darkness. He'd been up most of the night, unable to sleep. A bonus, considering he'd caught Laurel trying to slip away and had lured her back to bed. He'd reached for her again and again, but there was no getting his fill. He'd never, ever get enough of her, even if he spent every day of the rest of his life with her. Now she slept curled against his side, her palm resting over his heart.

A fitting position, considering she owned his heart and soul.

Sometime during the long hours he'd laid awake, he'd come to the stark realization that all his noble intentions had crumbled to nothing. Hearing her say she loved him had tipped him over the edge.

She stirred, her lashes brushing his chest as her eyes opened. She didn't say a word, didn't move. Sunrise began to filter murky light through the window, but they stayed where they were. He had no idea what she might be thinking, though he knew he couldn't let what he'd said the night before be the last conversation they had. She deserved the truth, at the very least. Then she could decide what she wanted.

"I can't do it." His voice emerged a low rasp, and she jerked against him.

"Do what?" She rolled to her back, and he propped himself on an elbow so he could look at her.

"Walk away from you."

Moisture pooling in her eyes, she swallowed hard. "Oh."

That was it, just *oh*. He didn't even know what to make of that, but it hadn't sounded particularly enthusiastic. "I should, you know. Walk away. My life is a hot mess. I'll just tie you down."

Her gaze met his, and anger sparked where the tears had been. "Did you ever think that might be what I need?"

He shook his head. The idea was as ludicrous as claiming a caged bird was better off never being allowed to fly.

"I've been flitting from one place to another most of my adult life." She fluttered her hand through the air. "I could use some roots, some place where I'm needed, people who love me unconditionally. The only person in the entire world who's ever felt that way about me is my older brother. My parents sure as hell don't."

"I do."

She snorted. "No, you care about me and will never forget me. That's nowhere near the same thing."

Locking his gaze with hers, he let her see everything he felt. No hiding, no more barriers. "I love you, Laurel. More than I ever thought I'd love another woman again. More than life itself." He glanced aside, confessing the fear that had really held him back. "I just think you should have someone less...burdened, less serious, more spontaneous and upbeat like you are."

"I've dated a lot of men like that, and I'm still single." Her eyebrows arched, an edge of frustration in her words. "Apparently, they aren't my type. Apparently, I fall in love with complicated, hot mess workaholics. No matter how hard I try not to."

God, he loved it when she said she loved him. He didn't think he could ever hear it often enough, even if she told him a million times. But love wasn't enough, was it? They both needed more. "I am a workaholic. Or I have been for a lot of years. It was one thing to immerse myself in work after the divorce—I just wanted to forget that my life was in shambles—but it's another thing to think I can keep that pace and still give my daughter what she needs now that she lives with me full-time. I've basically been setting myself up for failure."

A glimmer of hope shone in her eyes. "So you're cutting back?"

"Yeah, you were right." He lifted her hand to his lips, kissed her palm. "I don't need the money, and I don't have to say yes to every offer. I'm going to pick what I like to do best and delegate the rest."

The hope mixed with doubt. "Are you sure you can actually do that?"

He understood her skepticism. She knew him. She'd been there to see how he operated all summer. He was anything but easygoing and slowing down wasn't exactly in his vocabulary. At least not yet.

"Maybe...you can be there to remind me."

Her eyes slammed closed and a tear tracked down her cheek. "Don't do this to me, Neil. Don't jerk me around with this *it's over but I can't walk away, I love you but want you to be with someone else* garbage."

Fierce jealousy clawed at him. Yes, he thought she should have better than him, but the idea that she might really turn to another man made him want to put his fist through a wall. "I want the best for you because I love you. But I don't know that I'm what's best for you. I have another year, maybe a year and a half, before I make it through the contracts I've already signed. Vi and I are relocating our lives, and you'd better believe I'll be watching like a hawk to make sure nothing happens at her new school."

Resignation quashed whatever hope was left in her gaze when she met his eyes. "You don't have time for me. Of course."

"I'm trying to tell you what we're up against." He tightened his grip when she tried to tug her hand away. "I want you to understand what you'd be facing if you really mean it when you say you don't want our relationship to end. I wanted to give you the easy way out because I thought that was best for you."

"You don't want to give me the easy way out now?" she challenged, her lips flattening into a tight line.

"Fuck no!" Okay, not the most romantic turn of phrase, but her mouth relaxed enough to twist into a reluctant grin. "I was trying to do the right thing, and...God, if you hadn't actually said you loved me, I might have pulled it off."

She shook her head, her hair rustling against the pillowcase. "You had to know, deep down, how I felt."

"Denial is a powerful thing, sweetheart. I knew you cared." He winced at the insipid word. It tasted as bland rolling off his tongue as it had last night. "You said you wanted to continue seeing each other.

You said you loved me. I need you to know what that will mean for you, for us, at least for the next eighteen months. If you're willing to ride this out with me, then I'm selfish enough to let you. I never wanted to let you go, but I would have. For your sake."

She huffed out a derisive laugh. "For a smart man, you're an idiot sometimes."

"No arguments here." He waited tensely as she went silent. She searched his face for a long time, searching for...he didn't know what, but he hoped she found it.

"You swear you'll learn to delegate?"

"Once we move, I'm going to hire a personal assistant. I'll hire a temp as soon as I get back to LA. It'll free up some time, but an assistant can't write for me." He shrugged, offering a self-deprecating smile. "Also? You can kick my ass if I don't pick up this delegation thing fast enough. I'm guessing Vi will help you."

"Girl power." She nodded. "We have to stick together."

He brushed his lips over her palm again. "She told me to ask you to move in with us."

Her breath caught, those dark eyes going wide, so vulnerable it made his heart ache.

"I want that," he told her. "I want that so much. You and me and Vi, together as a family. If that's what you want too. Or we can go slower. Whatever works for you. Just...be willing to stick it out with me."

Her thumb rubbed over the back of his hand. "Are you still upset that she came to me with secrets and not you?"

"No. I know you're asking because we'd have to deal with that again if we stayed together." He'd made some peace about what happened with Violet. He didn't need to be a perfect father—he'd done his best to be there for her, and he knew she loved him. This wouldn't be her only big secret, and he had to accept, as Laurel had mentioned, that part of growing up was having his daughter try to figure things out on her own. Sometimes that would work well, and sometimes it would blow up horribly. Asking questions, being present and ready to listen when she wanted to talk was enough. Even then, he'd make mistakes as a parent. He could only apologize when he messed up and try to do better.

He looked at Laurel. "I'm glad Vi had someone she felt comfortable confiding in, and I'm glad that you clued me in on deeper problems so we could figure out a workable solution. She's maturing into a wonderful, responsible, ambitious young woman, and I'm proud of my part in helping her become the person she is and will be. I'll try to show her how to not take on too much, but everyone makes mistakes. Her, me, everyone." He sighed. "The perfectionist in me has to deal with that simple fact. I don't always like it, but I can deal."

"With the occasional minor flip out thrown in where you try to shove me out of your life." The words wobbled a bit, the hurt he'd caused stamped on her face.

"I'm sorry. I apologize. I was wrong." Between each sentence, he kissed her brow, her cheeks, the tip of her nose, her lips. "I'm sorry, and I love you. I'll never try to do what's best for you again, I swear."

The joke fell flatter than a pancake because her eyes welled with tears and her free hand slapped his chest. "*You* are the best thing for me. Get that through your thick skull, Graves."

"I'm trying." For her? He'd do damn near anything. "Until I believe that, why don't I just say I'd feel like the luckiest bastard in the world if you'd consider forgetting everything I said about breaking up?"

"I'll consider it." She drew in a breath. "You wanted to give me fair warning about your schedule and some of the big adjustments hitting your life." She looked down at their linked fingers. "I guess you deserve the same fair warning from me. Because of my history, I'm always going to be oversensitive about work taking precedence over family. I will call you on it if I think you're heading too far out into workaholic-land. I'll be too scared that letting things slide will mean there's no way back, and that I'd be giving you permission to put me last. You're going to have to deal with my paranoia, at least until I trust that, back in the real world, you really will make me a priority."

"That's fair. I'll do everything in my power to make sure you understand every single day just how important you are to me. I don't want you to let me get away with anything." He rested his forehead against hers, craving the closeness. "I'm probably going to need a few reminders after so many years of being chained to my deadlines. But I swear I'll discuss it with you before I agree to take on anything new, so you'll have a chance to speak up if you foresee a problem."

"Deal." She cupped the back of his head, and he felt her shaky exhalation against his skin. "I'm game if you are. I don't want to lose you, not without even trying."

There were a lot of important decisions ahead of them—like where to call home—but he figured as long as they could make those choices together, and kept choosing to prioritize each other, they might just make this last. It sounded pretty damn good to him, anyway. Then again, any future that had Laurel in it seemed right next door to heaven. He still wasn't quite convinced he deserved her, but he was smart enough to keep her.

Forever, if he had his way.

She fidgeted, and he leaned back to meet her eyes.

"If it's okay with you, I want to live in Half Moon Bay, near my brother. I don't want to miss my nephew growing up the way I did when I was traveling." She shrugged. "Especially since I know they want to have one or two more children. I want to be there, be part of their lives."

Well, that resolved one big uncertainty. Nice. "You're going to give Violet those cousins I've denied her."

"My brother will anyway." Mirth filtered through her voice. "But I'm happy to take credit."

Something shifted in her expression, her merriment fading. She glanced away, but not before he saw the questions in her gaze.

"What?" He tapped her chin. "Something else is on your mind."

Her lips twisted. "It'll bring up a sore point."

"Okay. I'm ready." He hesitated. "As long as you're not changing your mind."

"No, not at all." She squeezed his fingers tight. "And I want you to know that no matter how you answer this, I'm not going to change my mind. But if we're planning for the future…"

"Okay." But he couldn't help the way his muscles grew taut.

"Would you—" Her words seem to stall out. "Would you ever want to have more kids?"

"You mean if we got married?" Now that was a suggestion with promise.

She gave him a sideways glance. "Marriage isn't really a requirement for making babies, but sure…if we tied the knot, would you want more children? You made a pretty darn good one with Violet."

He smiled. "Yeah, I did, though Cara gets half the credit, of course."

"Of course."

The image of Laurel, round and ripe with his child, came unbidden to his mind. Equal parts desire and fear lanced through him. "If…if you wanted kids, I might be convinced to try having another one. I'd probably sweat bullets the entire pregnancy and be a nervous wreck."

"Understandably." Her expression softened and she laid a palm against his jaw.

He leaned into the contact and closed his eyes. God, he loved her.

"So, I would say...not opposed to more children, but it would be hard to risk going through that again. I'd be terrified that if something happened, I'd be shut out. I'd lose something that meant the whole damn world to me."

"We don't have to jump into anything," she assured him. "Once we survive your deadline madness, we can discuss it. I'll put it on the calendar twelve to eighteen months from now. Sooner, if you land a really bad-ass assistant who can manage the hell out of everything but your writing."

He liked how she said it—as a *when* and not an *if*. When they got through all his current contracts, they'd still be together and they'd have a future to plan. That was all he could really ask for. "I'll be sure to put bad-ass in the job description."

"You do that." She leaned up to pop a kiss on his mouth, but he followed her down for a longer, sweeter, more lingering affair.

They were both breathing hard when they came up for air. Damn, she got to him in the best possible way. "Well, there's only one thing left to do."

Her eyes crinkled at the corners. "Tell Violet I'm moving in with you?"

"Yep." He tucked her under him, mounting her in one smooth motion. "At breakfast, I think. She'll only just be coming out of hibernation then. Telling her sooner seems unfair."

Laurel looped her arms around his waist and grinned up at him. Love and need reflected back at him. "What will we do until then?"

He smiled. "All the good stuff."

ABOUT C. JORDAN

C. Jordan is a California native with an insatiable love for travel. When she's not writing sexy contemporary romance, she can usually be found working as a librarian or wandering the world with her husband.

ALSO BY C. JORDAN

Destination: Desire series

A Little Sinful

Never Let Go

Maybe This Time

Wild For You

Getting It Right

Forrester Brothers series

A Girl's Best Friend

The Girl Next Door

Unbelievable series

If You Believe

Believe in Me

Make Me Believe

Unbelievable anthology

Revved Up series

All Revved Up

All Tangled Up

Revved Up duology

want more?

Interested in free bonus epilogues, extended scenes, and short stories?

Members of C. Jordan's newsletter get access to all of these, plus exclusive sneak peeks at new projects and giveaways!

Join now at:

https://www.cjordanbooks.com/newsletter

EXCERPT FROM
ANYONE BUT YOU

Half Moon Bay, California

"**N**ora!"

The call from her elderly neighbor drew Nora Kirby up short before she'd made it inside her house. Her shoulders sagged. It was only noon, but she was bone-weary from a long night shift at the local hospital. All the nurses had a 3x12 schedule—three days on for twelve hours—but this shift had been especially rough, with a patient flat-lining on her twice. The man had pulled through, but without a heart transplant, his prognosis wasn't good. Sad, but there was little she could do except help keep him alive as long as possible. She'd been glad to hand him over to her replacement, was just as glad to be home, and even gladder she had four whole days to relax. She'd really been looking forward to collapsing on her couch and doing nothing for a while.

Instead, she turned back and pasted on a pleasant expression. "Hi,

Mrs. Hernandez. What's up?"

The other woman's wrinkled face creased in a grin as she walked across the lawn holding a box. "The mailman dropped off a package for you on my doorstep by mistake. All the way from Thailand. Isn't that strange?"

Considering Nora's older sister was currently vacationing there with her husband and infant son, it was hardly a shocker. Anne liked to send gifts from all the exotic locales she visited. She and her husband made their living as outdoor guides, though this trip was more of a working holiday.

Hurrying to take the package in case it was heavy, Nora smiled. "Thanks for bringing this over. It's from my sister."

"Ah, yes. The oldest one, *verdad*? So many girls and no boys. Your poor mother."

She shook her head at the familiar sentiment. Mrs. Hernandez was pretty old school about everyone preferring male children. Nora just let it slide. It wasn't worth getting into a women's lib argument with someone she rarely saw and would rather remain on good terms with.

"Four girls, actually. Anne, then me, Hazel, and Camille. I don't think my mom ever mentioned wishing for boys."

"*Sí*, but your mother is *muy loca.*" Mrs. Hernandez winked and trundled back over to her own porch.

Well, there was no arguing the older woman's point. Dinah Kirby *was* a level of drama queen that most people would see as batshit crazy, and that was putting it kindly. Nora pressed her lips together and marched into her house.

She set the box down on her kitchen table and dumped her purse next to it. Using the edge of one key, she opened the package. Almost a dozen flat tissue-wrapped bundles were nestled inside. A note sat on top, so she grabbed that and read it first.

Hey babe!

I just got back from a week in the Khorat Plateau where they hand-weave some of the most amazeballs silk you've ever seen in your life. I sent a silk scarf for each of my sister-friends. And, yes, there's even one for Mom. Be a doll and give them out for me. The post office here is a pain, so I just tossed them all in one box and shipped it to you. I threw in an extra scarf as a bribe for you dealing with the drama llama mama delivery.

Gabe and the munchkin say hello. Or Gabe does. My boy mostly just gurgles and looks adorable. But he'd say hello if he knew how!

Love you muchly. See you next month!

Anne

Nora made a face at the note. "As if one scarf is going to be enough for dealing with Mom. Anne, dear, you owe me big time."

She plucked out the two packages with her name on them and unwrapped the scarves. The colors and patterns were exquisite, and she couldn't help the little "ooh" that escaped her lips. One was pastel blue shot through with pale gold and the other was a rich navy, patterned in bold reds and pops of yellow. They both felt incredible under her palm as she stroked them.

Her cell rang, jolting her out of her lovefest with the silk. She fished her phone out of her purse and answered it. "Hello?"

"Hey, it's Karen."

One of Anne's best friends in the world. She'd also babysat Nora, Hazel, and Cami when they were young girls.

Nora tucked the phone between her shoulder and her ear. "Hi, hon. How's it going?"

"Good, good. I was wondering if you had a sec to go over some stuff for the baby shower?"

Nora bit back a groan. How, *how*, had she gotten herself roped into planning a double baby shower for two of her older sister's best friends? But she knew the answer—because Anne was in Thailand and couldn't plan it herself, and Nora was a sucker for the people she loved. Anne's friends had always been good to her, little pools of sanity and stability that helped keep her mother's crazy at bay.

After digging around in the box, she came up with the scarf labeled for Karen. "You know what? Why don't I come over and we can chat about it? I have a present here for you from Anne, and I will allow you to feed me lunch as a delivery fee."

Karen laughed. "Well, I'm lolling around like a beached whale since I went on maternity leave, but the nice lady my husband hired to chase our two sons around and occasionally throw food at our family made some amazing Swedish meatballs last night. We're having leftovers for lunch."

"Sold," Nora declared, heading for her room to change out of her scrubs. "I like any leftovers I didn't have to cook in the first place. Be there in twenty minutes."

"Great. I could use the company anyway."

Exactly eighteen minutes later, Nora was knocking on Karen's door. A sober-looking woman with iron-gray hair answered the door. "You must be Nora."

"That's right. And you must be the maker of amazing Swedish meatballs."

A small smile cracked the woman's façade. "They're my specialty."

"I can't wait to taste them then." Nora winked as she was waved into the house.

"Nora!" Karen sat in an easy chair by the fireplace, her feet propped on a stool. She held out her arms. "Forgive me if I don't heave myself up. That takes all of Tate's strength and a small crane."

"I'm sure your hubby is up to the challenge." Nora bent down for a hug, and felt the baby give a hard kick. "Are you sure we should have waited this long to hold the baby shower?"

"I'll make it to the shower, don't worry." Karen waved that concern away. "Besides, Julie's due date is a few weeks behind mine and it's her first."

Julie was another of Anne's best friends, another of Nora's childhood babysitters. It was nice to see her happily married and having a baby too.

After setting Karen's present on her lap, Nora retreated to another chair and sat. "Open it. I want to see what you think."

Without further urging, Karen shredded the tissue and pulled out the length of silk with a gasp.

"This is fantastic!" She wrapped the scarf around her neck, tying an artful knot. The light green on dark green was just the right combination to accent her emerald eyes.

"It's beautiful," Nora agreed. "Big sis picked great colors."

"What's beautiful?"

She tensed at the sound of that familiar, deep voice behind her. Ben Hudson, Karen's younger brother, who had been in the same grade as Nora in school. Unlike their sisters, they hadn't been close. At all.

"This." Karen pointed to her gift. "Anne sent it from Thailand."

"Hey, that is pretty awesome." He was carrying three plates, two stacked on a single brawny arm. He handed a dish to his older sister and popped a kiss on her cheek. Then he hooked a foot around the footstool in front of Nora's chair and pulled it away so he could sit on it. He handed her one of the remaining plates.

"Thanks." Nora couldn't help it if her tone was a bit grudging. Ben had been rubbing her the wrong way since junior high. Their older sisters had been best friends forever, so they were all thrown together at every family gathering. There was no real way for Ben and Nora to avoid seeing each other, but running into him unexpectedly wasn't her idea of a good time, especially when she'd been hoping for a relaxing gab session.

He caught her gaze and gave her a cheeky wink, which just made her stiffen. The jackass felt a compulsion to needle her every damn time he was near, and she had to suppress the urge to deck him. She offered him a stony stare and turned her attention to her food. The meatballs were as delicious as promised, but she would have enjoyed them more if he hadn't been there. His very presence bothered her.

Karen made a little humming noise of pleasure as she took a big bite of lunch. Ben glanced at his sister. "Your housekeeper-nanny lady needs a raise."

The siblings grinned at each other before diving back into the food. There was a definite family resemblance between the two—same nose, same jaw line, same brilliant green eyes. They even had the same ears. His face was a masculine version of hers, but that was where the similarities ended. Karen was a blonde and Ben was brunette. She was short and had curves that could put Marilyn Monroe to shame. He was tall and broad and had a voice so deep it seemed to resonate.

Nora had always thought he sounded a bit like James Earl Jones. She remembered when he'd had the cracking squeak of a tween, but when he'd hit puberty...hello, Vin Diesel bass. His voice unsettled her. It reached into her and stirred something she didn't want stirred.

She turned away, banishing those foolish thoughts. Ben Hudson had been a thorn in her side for over a decade. Thinking about his big body and deep voice changed nothing. Deep down, he was still the little jerk he had been all those years ago. Pushy, rude, obnoxious.

Setting her empty plate aside with a little groan, Karen rubbed her burgeoning belly.

Ben shook his head, staring with what looked like fascinated horror as her stomach rippled. "Man, you look so ready to pop. You're huge."

His sister blinked and Nora had to resist the urge to lean forward and smack him upside the head. Yep, still obnoxious and rude. "Oh my God, Ben. You have the sensitivity of a rock. You don't say things like that to pregnant women."

He waved an impatient hand. "Yes, let's all lie to women just because they're pregnant. That's feminist."

www.ingramcontent.com/pod-product-compliance
Lightning Source LLC
Chambersburg PA
CBHW031534310726
48971CB00008B/2480